DENYING THE DEVIL

MASTERSON COUNTY BOOK 4

CALLE J. BROOKES

PROLOGUE

His son was dead. Gone. A victim of his own stupidity and youth and baser urges. Clive understood that. He wasn't a stupid man, nor was he blind to the ways of the world. His boy Jay had never been the best sort, nor had he been the brightest.

Dog mean, some had said about his younger son. His *real* son. His blood.

Clint was just the bastard his wife, Paula, had foisted on him the day they'd wed. He'd given the boy his name out of duty and obligation. Because the father of that boy had been his own brother, who'd taken off into the hills when Paula had said she was pregnant. Women in Masterson,

Wyoming, were hard to come by. He'd taken the first woman he could stand talking to who knew her way around the bedroom.

He hadn't truly regretted it. Paula had been a riot to play with. Always up for an adventure in the sack, too.

Ovarian cancer had taken her out of the world, and his life, when the boy she'd given him had been all of sixteen months old.

He'd had the raising of Jay and his older step-son, Clint, ever since. Jay had made some missteps along the way, but Clive had never expected his boy to end up like *this*.

His boy hadn't deserved to suffer like he had there at the end. No human being did. Hell, not even a dog deserved this.

Jay had made mistakes, but his boy had died in pain. No amount of drugs could completely dull the pain of the burns that would never have healed. Or the pain of losing the girl Jay had wanted.

That it was his boy's fault for setting the fire mattered little.

Those damned Masterson boys should have gotten Jay out faster than they had. It would have been the right thing to do.

Why couldn't they have done the right thing to do?

Clive collapsed next to his son's hospital bed as the tears almost destroyed him.

Jay hadn't deserved to die this way. Not because of some damned girl. It just wasn't right. Jay had deserved better.

1

NATHANIEL MASTERSON, HEAD OF THE Masterson County Hospital, waited around the small ER until the woman he needed finally showed up. She'd been somewhere in the back of the small ward, helping with an MVA patient who'd needed her mother. The mother was currently in ICU with a very cautious prognosis.

It had been a longer night than he even wanted to think about. But everyone would live, barring any complications.

And he—*they*—still had a forty-minute drive to the ranches where they lived. He checked his watch. Nate had moved Persephone Tyler—his nemesis and thorn in side—to the later afternoon/early evening shift months ago. He'd had her on three p.m. to three a.m. but that had had to change.

It was just too dangerous for a woman to be out that late.

Even in Masterson County.

Recent events in the town that had nearly killed all three of his brothers—and all three of Perci's sisters—had made that abundantly clear to him.

Nate wanted Perci on the same shift he was on.

Easier for him to keep an eye on the little trouble magnet that way. Trouble just had a way of finding *her*.

She was the type of woman a smart man never turned his back on. That man had to keep his wits about him at all times.

Nate was stuck with her as a major part of his life; she was sister to all three of his sisters-in-law. He adored the three other Tyler women. There wasn't anything he wouldn't do for the women his brothers loved.

That meant Perci was *his* responsibility when at the hospital. More so than anyone else, though he took the safety of the rest of his staff seriously, as well.

But Persephone Tyler...Perci was *his* to watch over. He'd felt that way about her from the very beginning. Long before her sisters had captivated his brothers.

He'd known her and wanted her long before they had ever met her sisters.

Nate found himself wanting to watch her far more than a smart man should.

She dragged in, fatigue clear in her Tyler blue eyes. And limping. He'd heard the story—one of her patients tonight had had a massive seizure. The man was nearly as big as Nate; Perci had been knocked to the floor during the event. She'd done some damage to a not-quite healed fracture in her leg she'd suffered recently.

He'd told her a week ago she should have still been in the cast. But she'd insisted it come off.

She would never complain, especially to him. He called her name and motioned toward his of-fice door, right off the main lobby.

Her shoulders slumped and a wariness hit her face, but she nodded. Nate studied her as she limped toward him, clutching the crutch that one of the orthopedic physicians had insisted she use for a day or two. The physician had had a tough time getting her to agree—but he'd eventually managed. Nate had commiserated with the man an hour ago.

Perci eyed Nate like he was about to bite.

She felt about him the same as he felt about her. They were two tigers caught in a cage, ready to defend their small space from the other. Nipping and snarling, biting and clawing.

Perci rubbed her face with one hand. She was paler than normal. The freckles on her cheeks stood out like paint spots. "What is it, *sir?*"

She always called him that when they were on the clock; it was another one of her little ways of poking at the bear. Perci loved to poke the bear.

Nate was the damned bear, and he knew it.

"Inside my office. We have some *family* business to discuss."

"We're not *family*, Dr. Masterson. Not you and I. You're the one Masterson I'm not going to claim. How many times do I have to tell you that?"

"Ha ha. We're *kissing* cousins. You might as well get used to it." He'd like to kiss her. Just to stop that little mouth from snipping at him all the time.

But if he ever started kissing her, he'd probably never want to stop.

"Just because my sisters went all loony over a bunch of Masterson cowboys doesn't mean I'm as gullible. Trusting. Naive. Willing to be so stupid." Her smirk was weak. It had him mentally sighing. Why did she always have to *fight?* Especially him.

It seemed like they'd been fighting since the moment they'd met. She was tired and hurting, and still hissing like a half-wild kitten.

"You think your sisters made mistakes?" He knew she didn't; Perci was a strong supporter of her new brothers-in-law in everything. It was just Nate she didn't like.

His fault. He hadn't exactly gone out of his way to play nice with this woman. He'd done everything he possibly could to push her away.

"No. But only *three* of you brothers were good husband material. And they snatched them all up. Not everyone in a family can measure up." She shot him a sassy look, though the exhaustion in her face and in the way she held herself told him its own story. "I don't suppose you have a cousin somewhere for me? I met one or two at the weddings who would work."

He'd not wanted to admit it to anyone, but he'd

been worried about her tonight.

It hadn't been all that long ago that she'd been injured by a burning beam when a monster had attacked his brother and her identical twin. Perci's actions had saved all of their lives—and she'd ended up with second-degree burns on her back and a few broken bones. She was still healing.

Still looked so...vulnerable. Nate hated when Perci was vulnerable.

Her family had had its share of troubles in the past year. That, no one could deny.

What he had to tell her would just wrap all that up. Tie the loose ends. Hopefully, the Tylers could move on after that.

Like Perci's three sisters Phoebe, Pip, and Pandora, all had.

Sparring with Perci just hadn't been the same since the night Jay Gunderson had burned down the Tylers' barn, with Perci, Pip, and Nate's brother Matt inside.

"Jay Gunderson is dead. Complications from an infection. I thought you deserved to know as soon as I learned."

Perci stared at him out of those eyes of hers that he still dreamt about. "I'm not exactly sure what I am supposed to say here."

"I know." The loss of life, any life, had always struck him hard. But in this instance, he just couldn't force himself to mourn the man who had tried to kill the woman in front of him. Who had tried to kill Matt. And Perci's twin, Pip, who had never hurt anything or anyone in her entire life. "But I wanted you to hear it from me."

She nodded. "Thank you. I'll tell Dad."

"I've already called Matt to let him and Pip know."

She nodded again. "Of course. Just what she needs. Reminding of Jay Gunderson. She's not feeling well today."

"You spoke with her?"

"No." It was a simple answer, but Nate didn't press. He knew how she operated. And damn it all, even though it belied all logic, Perci always seemed to know exactly how her identical twin was feeling. Especially since Pip had announced her pregnancy. "But I know."

"That's a little too woo-woo for me."

"Your powers of description are awe inspiring, Dr. Nate."

He snorted. "Grab your things, smart ass, and let's go. I promised Matt and Joel I'd drive you home tonight."

"Gee, thanks, Galahad."

But she followed along. Which told him her exhaustion went deeper than her desire to avoid him at all costs.

She said very little as they drove. About twenty minutes into the drive, he looked over at her. She hadn't spoken in a while.

"You ok?"

"Just thinking. Tired. Dr. Paterson gave me something for the pain. It's getting to me."

"Admitting a weakness? You must be hurting worse than I thought?" All joking aside, he wanted to know.

She went silent and stayed that way until they got to his home. He hadn't intended to bring her there, but he had.

Perci hadn't said a word when he'd made the turn into the private access road that would lead to his place, instead of going past it on toward the Tyler ranch several miles beyond.

It wasn't until they were in his driveway and he'd rounded the front of the car that he realized she'd drifted off.

Nate made a quick decision. She didn't need to be putting weight on that foot. Not when she didn't have to.

He opened her door and leaned down.

Startled blue eyes met his. "Nate?"

"Yes."

"Why am I here?"

"I made an executive decision—as your physician."

"Dr. Paterson treated me tonight."

"He gladly turned your care over to me after you snipped at him tonight. So...I made a decision. You're sleeping here tonight. Where I can keep an eye on you."

"It's just a sprain, you dork."

"And it happened on my watch. You're stuck with me tonight. *Unless* you can get Pan or Levi to drive you home? It is rather late..."

She sighed, then turned her face against his neck. He half feared she'd bite him. "I can walk, Masterson. I'm not helpless."

"Can it. You're dead on your feet. And probably a bit wobbly. You should have two crutches, not one. The instant I put you down, you'll fall and break your neck. Sue the shit out of us."

"Right. Like I'd sue my three brothers-in-law—how would they support my future nieces and nephews?" She squirmed. "Put me down, you idiot."

"No." Nate knew he was being a contrary ass, but she'd acted like he was a serial killer out to carry her off. Besides, he was enjoying it. Perci smelled like all woman. The scent of hospital antiseptic and cleaner was still there, but he could make out her shampoo, too. And the unique scent that was all *her*. "It's raining, and you'll fall flat on your ass—or break that leg again."

He wasn't an idiot. His attraction to this woman was stronger than any he'd ever had for another woman.

Perci was the woman he would dream about at night for a long, long time.

Sometimes that attraction got the best of him, and he did something stupid like this.

He scooped her up and carried her over the steps and onto the front porch.

The door opened, and his brother Levi stepped out. "Caught you a pretty fish, too? *Finally*. I told my wife you were the slowest on the uptake."

Levi's words had deepened with satisfaction at the word *wife*. All of his brothers sounded just like that when they mentioned the women they loved. Matt and Pip were now fully ensconced on their ranch a mile or so past the entrance to this one that

Nate currently shared with Levi. This one had been the family homestead for generations. Levi ran the ranch—all the properties, mostly—owned by the Mastersons, while Nate's brother Joel ran the county as sheriff, and Matt ran a successful vet practice and worked toward building his own horse ranch. Joel and his wife, Phoebe, lived a bit closer to the town now, having finished redoing the old homestead that had been Nate's grandparents' place. There was one smaller chunk of property with a three-story, four bedroom home on it. It was about five miles west of where he now lived. Levi owned two of those miles in between. Matt owned one, and Nate owned the rest.

One day, if Nate ever married, he'd take his own wife there. He was almost finished with the renovations now.

It was just a matter of another week or two.

He'd been thinking of moving there a lot lately. Hard not to do, when his house was constantly filled with his brothers and the women they loved. Redheaded, blue-eyed women everywhere he turned. Each and every one of them reminding him of the one in his arms.

Perci was always around now, too. Never far from her sisters. They traveled as a damned pack;

that was for certain. Every time he blinked, she was there.

Tempting him to do something completely stupid. Like touch her. Kiss her.

Give her his entire soul.

"Can it, Levi. She's exhausted and took a hard knock tonight when a patient fell on her. Hurt her ankle and leg again. I just gave her a lift. She's had some pain meds and is extremely groggy."

"Sure, you did." Levi smirked at him, then looked at Perci more closely. "She looks more like a captive. That your intention? Carry your woman away? Let me guess, taking Persephone down to Hades? I was going to try it with Pandora if she didn't start cooperating, but I figured she'd emasculate me if I even tried. I *thought* Perci was the scariest sister, but I've learned. Pan has her beat hands down."

"He's lucky I don't have a scalpel."

PERCI WAS JUST GLAD IT WAS SO DARK HER brother-in-law couldn't see the red on her cheeks. Levi was the type to snark at her for what his brother was doing. And what in the hell *was* Nate doing? "I can walk. He just likes to lord it over me that he's bigger and stronger and in charge—at the hospital. I *thought* he was driving me home."

"Aha. He captured you when you were least expecting it. I'm not going to ask what Hades is planning to do with you, Persephone, but I can imagine."

"Ha ha, Levi." She thought about squirming again. But the arms around her were far too strong for that to do much good. She would just keep her dignity and let this play out how it would. That was all she could do.

But, damn it, she did feel like a captive.

With Nate, it was best to just let him *think* he was winning. She'd just do that until he decided to let her down.

Sometimes it stunk, having him so much bigger than she was. Perci suspected Nate liked the size difference. Liked having her vulnerable and in his clutches.

Hell, that drug was making her a bit too dramatic tonight. She squirmed slightly, but the arms around her were hard and strong. She wasn't getting down until he chose to *put* her down. Period.

He smiled down at her, but there wasn't any humor in the expression.

More like a mountain lion about to pounce. That was usually how she felt about the man. Like he was going to attack her at any moment.

Past history had told her she wasn't that far off the mark with him. Give him an opportunity, and he definitely would pounce.

"You can put me down, Masterson."

"Nope. It's a matter of principle, now."

"Excuse me?" The man didn't make a lick of sense. Except that he'd always enjoyed making her life as difficult as he possibly could. She squirmed again. His arms tightened.

Nate had really strong arms that she knew would never drop her, at least. There was that. The man was going to keep her safe—all while annoying the hell out of her.

"Inside. Then you can camp out in the guest room. If you really want, I'll drive you home in a bit. Your dad home tonight?"

She shook her head. Her dad had been splitting his time between his partner's ranch in Texas and theirs, lately.

"The boys?"

"No. Phoebe and Joel have them," Levi answered. "So our sweet little Perci would be left all alone over there."

"Exactly."

Her younger sister Pan snickered when he walked by her. She'd been the one to flick on the light. "Watch out, Perci. You're next."

"Bite me, Pandora. Just because the rest of you lost what brain cells you have the instant you saw a Masterson doesn't mean *I* will."

"*Sure*, you won't. I'll get you some pajamas."

"Gee, thanks." She hated feeling helpless like this. No doubt he knew exactly that.

He carried her down the hall, then dumped her on the mattress of the guest room.

Ok, so maybe he lowered her gently, but...the idea of Nate leaning over her while she was on a bed had her breath catching and something tightening in her gut.

"I'm perfectly capable of staying alone for one night." But she didn't like it—and would never admit that to anyone. Except maybe her twin.

She hadn't spent more than half a dozen nights alone in her life.

"No doubt. Good thing it's just for one night, right?"

He smirked.

Perci wanted to smack him. Nate could be such an ass sometimes.

2

NATE COULD TELL BY THE EXPRESSION IN those Tyler blue eyes that she was royally pissed at him. And mortified. He hadn't meant to do that, but she'd hurt herself, it was late, and she would be all alone, miles from civilization.

Not an idea he was comfortable with.

Tyler women had a habit of attracting trouble. It just wasn't going to happen. She'd been hurt on his watch; that mattered to him. And not just because it was *her*. "Sorry if I embarrassed you. That wasn't my intention."

"And just what was? Shoving down my throat that you're bigger and *in charge* of every little thing? Well, you've accomplished that. So here I am, captive in your guest room. Now what?"

He ignored the bite in her tone. He had to admit it—she deserved to be irritated at him this time. He had stepped over the line with her. Again. "I'm going to take one more look at that ankle, then I'll get out of your hair. You can put hemlock in my oatmeal in the morning, or something. Then we'll be even."

"Hemlock? Seriously?" Her eyes narrowed, and the spark that was Perci returned in an instant. He hadn't even realized it had been mostly missing lately...until that moment.

"Don't witches carry that with them everywhere? To trap unsuspecting men? The way the rest of your little coven nabbed my idiot brothers?"

Her body tensed against his. He covered his grin by turning away. At least angry, she wasn't embarrassed any longer.

He shouldn't needle her, but he somehow always ended up doing exactly that.

"Funny, Masterson. I think it was the other way around. My sisters *used* to be reasonable, rational, intelligent women until your brothers seduced the lot of them."

"If there was any seducing done, you Tylers

are responsible. With those eyes, those lips. The hair..." The hair of hellfire. He brushed his fingers over her braid. It always surprised him that her hair was so cool and soft to the touch.

It should burn. That made the most sense.

Persephone Tyler made *him* burn hotter than hell.

And she always had. Since the moment his mother had hired her to work as a nurse with the small hospital his mother had run for most of his life. Now that hospital was *his* responsibility. As was *she*.

Hell, he wished he was as stupid as his brothers sometimes. As reckless. Wished he could just lower her to the bed—in the room *next* door— and show her exactly what she did to him. Keep her in his bed until he'd extinguished every flame she lit in him.

Not because he was a Masterson and she was a Tyler and everyone just expected they'd be to-gether eventually, but because *he* had burned for this woman from the very moment he'd looked up at the new nurse his mother had hired. Every nerve in his body had jumped to full alert.

She hadn't stopped burning him since.

He'd wanted Perci Tyler since *long* before his

three brothers had fallen hard for her sisters. Temptations, the lot of them.

Sirens luring unsuspecting men to their doom.

"Take off the cast. Let me have a look."

"Maybe I don't want you looking at my leg? Maybe my feet stink? Maybe I haven't shaved in a month?"

"I've seen worse—I think I'll survive." He reached for the brace himself and removed it gently.

There wasn't a damned thing he could do for her ankle that the staff at the hospital hadn't already done, and they both knew it.

Nate just wanted to touch her for a minute.

It was time he admitted it to himself—he was never *not* going to be burning for her.

She'd captured him, same as her three sisters had captured his brothers. That probably wasn't going to change anytime soon.

He'd been thinking lately that maybe it was time he finally did something about how he felt.

Nate brushed his fingers over the smooth skin of her calf—despite her claim, the skin was silky smooth—checking for excess swelling. "Does this hurt?"

She shivered.

Not the response he'd expected.

Nate jerked his head up, just in time to see a look of heat in the blue eyes he dreamed about almost nightly.

An almost *hunger*.

His fingers tightened on her skin. His other hand came up, and he cupped her cheek. Stupid move, no doubt, but he wasn't the kind to back down when he'd made a choice. "Baby? Did I hurt you?"

She didn't speak, just shook her head. Watched every move he made.

Hell, he wanted to touch her. Every soft, perfect inch of her.

Nate knew he shouldn't, but there was no damned reason why he couldn't at least *taste* her in that moment, was there?

Nate leaned forward and pressed his lips to that smart little mouth that had tempted him daily for months.

Perci met him halfway.

Oh, heaven help her. Nate Masterson was actually kissing her. Worse, why in the hell was she kissing the man back? Perci knew she should push the man away before something stupid and life altering happened. Mastersons were devils capable of turning Tyler women into wishy-washy idiots. She had three cases of living proof that she could draw on for that conclusion. Perci understood it. How could she not?

Kind, intelligent, strong, handsome, loving, beautiful men who loved her sisters like they'd hung the moon—it was no wonder her sisters were ridiculously, deliriously happy.

Her hands had a will of their own. They crept up around those broad shoulders and clung. She wanted to blame the pain killer she'd been given, but that was stupid. She was *choosing* to do exactly what she was doing right now. Nate was the biggest of his brothers. His shoulders were the widest, the strongest.

Perci fought the urge to purr as she felt just how perfectly the man was built.

Nate was the most beautiful man she had ever seen—and she'd freely admit that to anyone who asked—but when he opened his mouth to speak, he totally ruined everything.

She'd better get herself figured out before what they were about to do got her damned to this devil and back.

Once she gave in to him, there would be no escaping him.

No pomegranates, no temptations, needed.

She needed to remember that. Nate Masterson was the *devil* where she was concerned. He'd do anything to trap her into a stupid mistake.

He pulled away slightly. "Kiss me back."

Then his lips were on hers again, and he was practically devouring her.

Perci's hands went around his neck and—heaven help her—she kissed him right back.

3

He had been waiting forever to kiss this woman. Nate took the taste of her he wanted, suspecting it would be the only chance he got. Once she pushed him away, he'd probably never get to touch her again. Not with all the history between them.

She tasted like heat. Fire. Temptation.

No surprise at that.

He wanted to kiss her for longer—forever—but at the sound of light footsteps in the hall, he pulled back. "Pan is coming."

She gasped and jerked away, her eyes wide.

He stepped away from the bed deliberately.

"We'll...talk later. Good night, Persephone. I'll see you in the morning."

Nate passed his youngest sister-in-law in the hallway. She held pajamas in her hands and a toothbrush. No doubt they were going to talk for a while. All of the Tyler sisters were extremely close. It wasn't the first time Perci had stayed the night at his home. After she'd been released from the hospital when she'd been injured by Jay Gunderson, she and Pip had stayed where Nate and her sisters could keep an eye on both of them. For a time, they'd had all four sisters under this roof. Phoebe and Joel had been married, Pan had been their housekeeper until she'd married Levi, and Pip had barely left Matt's room until they were both healed.

But Perci had left as soon as she could. Almost ran to get away.

It had pissed him off for three days. He'd told himself it was because he hadn't felt that she was physically healed enough to return home, but that had just been his excuse.

He'd wanted Perci in his home. He wanted her on the same schedule as he was at the hospital—she'd gone back to work the week before she'd left his home—and in *his* home.

It hadn't helped that half of her intended medical leave had been spent working on that damned movie of Rowland Bowles's. The director had used body doubles when needed, due to Perci's cast. A lot of the filming had taken place either on his family ranch—or hers.

Nate had been a front-row spectator for a lot of it.

She'd made a beautiful fairy princess, perfect and fiery.

And every day he'd gone to his own bed to dream about her.

His brothers knew. They'd known from the moment they had first met Perci. And they'd understood.

His brothers had been just as susceptible to her sisters. Only *they* had caved in. And now his idiot brothers were beyond happy.

It was just *him* who wasn't.

Nate had known that from the moment Levi and Pan had said 'I do.'

The movie crew was back in Hollywood, working on post-production tasks that Nate didn't care about. But the fairy princess was still around. Still driving him crazy.

Making him dream. Making him want.

He had yet to decide what he was going to do about her.

He had to do something. He couldn't go on like this. Seeing her, wanting her, not touching her. She was going to be around for a damned long time, thanks to their siblings. Either he left Masterson, and everything he loved, behind.

Or he faced up to the inevitable.

And found a way to get exactly what he wanted from her. Somehow.

"Your lips are all red."

Pandora—Pan, for short—was staring at her like she was a bug. Pan—whose own lips were swollen. No doubt from kissing that husband of hers. They'd only been married a little over three weeks, but Pan was acting like she knew everything there was to know about men. Sex.

Pan had been a virgin until Levi. What could her sister really *know*?

Of course, if Levi kissed anything like his older brother Nate, Pan had probably caught up pretty quickly. Perci resisted touching her mouth.

She could still taste him.

"So? Did he kiss you?"

Her sister was pretty shrewd. Pan was the most diabolical—and probably smartest—of her siblings. Perci knew better than to even think about lying. Pan would see right through it. Besides, she didn't lie to her sisters if she could help it. She kept no secrets—except one.

They'd had almost absolute trust between them for years. Since Pip had been attacked at nineteen, since their mother had died shortly after leaving their family so deeply in debt they'd nearly drowned, and since the Masterson brothers had entered their world.

The Mastersons had brought nightmares—with Phoebe almost drowning in a flooded river, Pip and Perci almost burning to death in the barn, and Pan almost being killed by a madwoman—but the brothers had made her sisters beyond happy.

Perci adored every one of her new brothers-in-law for how they loved her sisters.

But through them, she'd gotten Nate. She still didn't know how she felt about that.

"He kissed me."

Pan smirked. "Of course he did."

"Shut up. I'm not going to get involved with Nate, Pan. I'm not. No matter what the rest of the family—or this town thinks. It's just not going to happen, so quit looking at me that way."

4

PERCI ESCAPED EARLY THE NEXT MORNING, catching a ride to her house with Phoebe and Joel, who'd stopped by for breakfast. Joel waited until she'd changed into clean scrubs, then drove her to the hospital.

Thankfully, this brother-in-law wasn't the teasing type. He didn't say a word about Nate.

Perci had almost thought her day was going to be uneventful. Until she was working the intake desk while Tiff took her lunch.

She looked up when the pneumatic doors slid open with the familiar hum. A dark-haired older woman in an expensive pantsuit stood there, looking around.

Perci knew exactly who the woman was.

Nate's mother walked right in like she owned the hospital—which as far as Perci knew, she still did—and came straight to the desk.

To Perci.

Like Perci had been her target all along.

She had the same eyes as her son. The color and shape were exactly like Nate's. So was the rich dark hair. She smiled at Perci across the intake desk. "Hello, Persephone, how are you?"

"Dr. Masterson, I'm doing...well." She didn't have any idea what she was supposed to say to the woman who was now her sisters' mother-in-law. She'd only met Rhea Masterson once, when she'd interviewed Perci for her current position. The woman had been calm, no-nonsense, and professional.

Her eyes had looked through Perci like she could see right through her and read every thought she'd ever had.

"You've healed all right? Compound fracture of the tibia?" Rhea's gaze dropped to the cast still on Perci's leg.

"Yes, ma'am. I bumped it last night when a patient fell on me. Nate and Dr. Peterson are being cautious. I'll be out of it within a week."

"Good. See you don't overdo it, dear. Is my son around?" She smiled, revealing an expression just like her son Levi's. "None of the boys know I've made it back. I'd like to surprise them."

"Nate's in his office, as far as I know." She'd made it a point to avoid him since The Kiss That Changed Everything, as she'd been calling it to herself. Whenever she thought about it. Which was far too often for her peace of mind.

They'd passed twice in the hallways, but he'd been with other people. He hadn't said a word. But she'd felt his gaze on her.

"Great. I'll sneak back and surprise him. Are you free for lunch?"

"Yes..."

"Good. We'll go to the diner. I've been craving those onion rings for days. Ever since I decided to come home."

As far as Perci knew, her sisters' mother-in-law had been out around the country doing medical relief after natural disasters. Rhea had been flooded in for Phoebe's wedding, had a recently broken arm and sprained knee for Pip's, and was dealing with a measles epidemic in Mexico for Pan's.

Her sons had been disappointed she'd not

been there, but they'd also joked about it. Apparently, if she *could* have been there, she would have. And they'd been secure in that knowledge.

But why on earth did she want to have lunch with *Perci*? Surely, she didn't believe the hype about Perci and Nate being involved?

Half the town thought they were, no matter what she had said to the contrary.

She had no idea how to deal with that man. Nate confused her on so many levels.

Part of her just wanted to pick up and run away. But that was the coward's way—Tylers did not *run* when things got bad. Period.

5

NATE'S DOOR OPENED. HE LOOKED UP, READY to rip into whomever had violated his privacy. The words died on his lips. "Mom! I didn't know you were coming home." He rose, ready to hug her.

She held up a hand to stop him. "Just what have you been up to? I'm hearing rumors about you and that pretty nurse out there? World War III Hospital Edition, is that what it's being called?"

He winced. "Where did you hear that from?"

"I don't know; half my friends tell me something's going on with the two of you. Yet I hear nothing about it from you—or my other sons."

"Perci and I...we don't exactly get along. That's all it is. People are making more of it than is actually there. How long are you here for?" He was not going to discuss Perci with his mother. Period. He wasn't discussing Perci with anyone, especially before he had how he felt for her fully figured out.

"As long as I am needed. I understand I have a sweet little daughter-in-law who's going to make me a grandmother soon and isn't feeling well. She'll need some pampering. Someone who understands what she'll be going through. I want to meet her as an adult—I delivered her and her sister, after all. I delivered *all* the Tyler girls. Every last one of the Tyler girls in this county, I believe. I'm here to help."

He winced internally. Pip was three months pregnant—it was going to be a long visit then. Nate loved his mother, but she could be intense. Meddlesome—especially when she thought it was best for her sons. That meant she was going to be staying.

He hoped his sisters-in-law were ready for the tornado about to invade them all. "We've missed you, Mom. I'm glad you're back."

"Glad to be back. Now. I'm going to go grab that beautiful little nurse out there. Take her to lunch. I'm sure she can fill me in on how well you've run my hospital since I've been gone."

Nate winced.

The idea of his mother and Perci possibly teaming up together against him absolutely terrified him.

NATE MASTERSON'S MOTHER TERRIFIED HER. Perci knew that two minutes after Rhea dragged her the mile down to the cafe. The owners had replaced the window that had been destroyed when John Rutherford had tried to kill Pan—and almost *had* killed her cousin Nikki. It made Perci leery to sit in one of those window seats ever again.

After they ordered, and Mrs. Masterson spoke to several people in the town, Nate's mother stared at her. "Well. *Now* we can talk. Woman to woman."

"Yes." Tylers were not cowards, she wasn't about to be afraid of this woman. Perci wouldn't let herself be. Now *confused*...that was a better word. "Can I ask, why did you invite *me* to lunch today? You could have asked any of your sons, and Pip is over at Matt's clinic right now."

"Because it's *you* that concerns me."

"Excuse me?"

"I know you and Nate are struggling together. I am here to help. He always has been a contrary boy."

"We're not... I mean...there's nothing...Nate and I just don't get along, that's all." How was she supposed to tell Nate's mother exactly how the man twisted her into a thousand knots?

She smiled softly. "I know. But I was also there the first time he saw *you*. It's one of the reasons why I left."

"Excuse me?

"I left to get out of his way." Rhea waved a hand dismissively. "He would never have gotten involved with a woman he worked with if I was around and in charge of everything. I left, thinking the two of you would work closely together and things would evolve. That's how I planned things, anyway."

Perci took a sip of her soda. Mostly to buy herself some time to come up with a response. The older woman *had* left rather abruptly all those months ago. Everyone had talked about it. No one had known why. They'd assumed it had something to do with the memories of her husband. Apparently, they'd all been wrong. "I'm sorry, but that doesn't make any sense."

"Yes, it does. Nate is the type of man to resist any kind of change in his life. He fights from morning until night because of that fear. I knew when he saw you, you'd give him the greatest fight of all. I honestly hadn't expected the fight to last *this* long, though. I was not planning to stay away as long as I did."

"That's...crazy. Nate and I...it's just never going to happen."

Yet she'd kissed him back, not even a full twenty-four hours earlier.

"You sure about that? I do have to admit I'm surprised—and thrilled—that my other three sons found their own happiness, with your sisters. I never expected *that* to happen. And now I'm going to be a grandmother. That's why I came back, instead of giving you and Nate more time. I can think of only one thing more perfect—and that is for my Nate to get his head out of his ass. So tell me: any ideas on how to help him do just that?"

Perci just sat there and stared.

She'd thought Nate was a piece of work. He didn't hold a candle to his mother.

6

PERCI MANAGED TO KEEP HERSELF TOGETHER with Rhea Masterson only because her mother had raised her to be able to handle herself in any situation with grace and dignity. She might spit and fight when called for, but Perci knew how to behave.

Perci wondered if Nate's mother did.

The woman was just too sly for her liking. Too all-knowing. It was irritating as hell.

Much like her son.

The idea that Rhea had taken off and missed almost a year of her sons' lives just so *Perci* and Nate would get together was insane.

And not something Perci was going to be sharing anytime soon.

Her shift ended. Her little red car was waiting. It had been vandalized a while back when one of her sisters had been attacked, but it had been fixed by one or two of her brothers-in-law. She wasn't getting rid of that car anytime soon, though. It had once been her mother's. She appreciated it, of course. But every time she drove that car she was reminded of the hell they had all been through on the mountain that day.

Phoebe had come so close to dying—and Perci and Pip hadn't been that far off, either.

It had changed them all that day.

Changed everything.

Her father was gone when she pulled in at the house. As were the boys; no doubt they were off somewhere with her sister. Phoebe had once been responsible for their brothers' care. Now at almost seventeen, twelve, and eight, the boys were either with their father of the evening or Perci. Phoebe still came over every day to tend the house and oversee the boys' homeschool lessons. They lived too far out of town to make public school a good option.

Until recently, Tylers kept to themselves.

Remnants of the hell they'd gone through since Perci had been nineteen and the sheriff's son had attacked her twin.

He had come back not even three months ago to harass them again. It had nearly proven fatal.

Perci would never forget that. She had the scars to remind her of Jay Gunderson and the hell he had brought them all.

He'd been in her bedroom at least once that she knew.

Something else she hadn't forgotten. She'd taken some of her spare cash—a rare occurrence in the Tyler family—and purchased paint and some new secondhand furniture for her space. Frivolous or foolish, maybe, but she'd needed to do it. To erase the taint of evil that she hadn't been able to forget.

She had the entire second floor of the house to herself now. Pip was gone, Phoebe was gone, Pan was gone. Even their younger brother Phoenix was gone, having followed the film crew back to California when they'd left. The house that had once seemed so full of life, love, people was barely that anymore.

Even her three youngest brothers were gone

more often than not, splitting their time between their sisters' places. With the Mastersons.

Her dad spent a great deal of his time working on his Hail Mary plan to save their ranch—in Finley Creek, Texas.

Perci pushed aside the melancholy and checked the doors one more time. Just to be on the safe side.

It seemed like she'd been afraid of her own home since the moment those assholes had attacked Phoebe.

But tonight. Tonight, it just seemed so much worse.

7

THAT NURSE WAS AS BEAUTIFUL AS HER sisters. He could see why his boy had been so enamored of her twin. Enamored enough to do some pretty stupid shit to get the twin's attention.

It had cost Jay his life.

Clive didn't know what he was doing there alongside the road, waiting for her again.

He'd followed that nurse home tonight. He'd seen her car when she'd pulled onto the small highway that led toward the edge of the county where all the Tylers lived. And he'd followed. Just like that.

Like he had all those times before.

Possibly just like Jay had the girl's twin.

Had his son watched the twin and just wondered what she was doing? Imagined taking her clothes off and taking her to her bed nearby?

Maybe. Maybe by following this girl he could understand his son's fascination. Understand why Jay had come after her again after three years in jail. There had to be something about those girls that had been worth dying for. There had to.

Otherwise, Jay's death made no sense at all.

Clive could walk up on that Tyler porch, burst through the door, and take that girl. Just take her, kill her, and leave her in a damned field somewhere her family would never find her.

Make those Tylers and Mastersons *pay* for the way they had taken his Jay from him.

Clive just stared as the lights inside the Tyler ranch told him exactly where the girl was. Perci. Her name was Perci. He'd known her for years now. Had made a point of making sure she knew *him*.

Perci had been in the barn that day with his boy.

He'd heard she'd almost burned alive. That she'd saved her twin's life. That she was a heroine. That she'd almost died.

Like his son had.

But she was fine now, had made a damned movie, and was screwing around with the fourth Masterson brother. A doctor.

They'd marry soon. Have kids of their own. Perfect children who wouldn't screw up to the same extent that Jay had. The Mastersons had old money, lots of land, and owned the damned hospital, as well.

She would prosper. While his son turned to dust. While Clive's dreams for his son did, as well.

Clive's phone buzzed. He checked it quickly.

It was Maria. His stepson—and nephew—Clint's neighbor. She thought it was getting her in good with Clive, letting him know what was going on with the boy. Maria thought Clive would care that his wife's granddaughter was growing up without a mother. Just like her two boys had. But that child wasn't any relation of Clive's other than a great-niece—he was no damned grandfather to that child, and he and Clint had both agreed on that.

But he hadn't told Maria that.

Not with him wanting a warm body in his bed at night. Maria was more than willing.

What would Maria think if she knew he was

outside this redheaded girl's home, staring at her silhouette through the window shade?

Probably nothing good.

Just like his son Jay had been.

Nothing good.

Damn it, why had Jay been so *stupid?*

Clive stayed exactly where he was as the hours passed.

Staring at her bedroom window and wondering what about her and her sisters had been worth his son dying over.

As the sun rose over the mountains, he was no closer to getting those answers.

8

NATE FOUND THE WOMAN HE WANTED IN THE back of the ER, treating a fair-haired child, long past the time she should have clocked out and headed home. He took one look at the patient chart and winced.

It was a child they had seen far too many times before. Nate would be consulting with the physician on duty about her impressions. He suspected abuse but wanted a corroborating physician's report.

Then he'd be calling the next stage in the process. He stood in the exam bay and watched Perci comfort the little girl as best she could.

The mother wasn't anywhere to be seen. And the father most likely hadn't even made an appearance.

Nate suspected the father was the one responsible for the girl's bruises in the first place. Perci looked up when he entered. The little girl, Ivy, stared at him out of fearful green eyes. Her little hand rose and she stuck her thumb in her mouth as her other hand tightened on Perci's scrub top. Perci wore scrubs with Cookie Monster printed all over the cotton. The blue of the puppet matched her eyes perfectly.

And the character no doubt helped soothe the children who came through the ER.

Perci somehow always got the child patients.

Perci was singing. Rocking. Holding the little one like it was the most natural thing in the world.

He could see her rocking her own child in just that way some day. Rocking her child as that child's father stared at them, thinking just how damned lucky he was.

That thought had him jolting.

Some other man would give her that child one day. Build a family, build a *life* with her. Change everything.

Nate scowled. The idea of some other man touching her pissed him off.

Nate wanted it to be *his* hands on her.

Hell, he wanted it to be his child she held just like that. And no other man's.

He was such a damned caveman where Persephone Tyler was concerned. She'd figure that out one day.

"Dr. Masterson, how can Ivy-bear and I help you this evening?" There was strain on her face. Her eyes kept flickering between him and the child. And the door. As if she expected the parents to walk in at any moment.

He somehow doubted that would happen. The mother wasn't exactly a prize. The father didn't even come close to being Father of the Year.

"Documentation." He kept his words low, not wanting to frighten the child. She was already seriously frightened of men in general. "I'm calling Joel's office and child protective services in five minutes. I need to speak with Dr. Hayes. And I need someone to take photographs."

She nodded. "I'll grab the camera."

"No, I'll get it. You just keep holding her." Keep doing what she was doing. It was working. The little girl was calming.

It was a long process, to document every mark and bruise on the little girl's body. They called in both the attending physician and the charge nurse to sign and witness. When it was finished, he excused himself to make the calls.

His brother Joel was far more helpful than the child protective services.

They gave a host of excuses. It was too late, the roads were too flooded, and unless an approved bed became available, Ivy was going to an institution first thing in the morning. An institution with troubled kids more than four times the not-quite-three-year-old's age.

It took some arguing on his part, some threats from Joel, and a whole lot of traded IOUs before a solution more in Ivy's favor was suggested and agreed on.

Nate and his brothers had been approved as emergency foster parents for teenage boys two years ago when one of their after-school hands had run into some family trouble. Edward had stayed with them for a full year before he'd graduated and left for college. The brothers' licensing was still current. With a few modifications and negotiations, it was agreed that Ivy would be coming home with Nate.

To Levi and Pan's official custody.

Nate winced. He should probably have at least mentioned it to the two first.

But his younger brother and sister-in-law would just have to make do.

He wasn't about to let that little girl—the little girl *he* had delivered—disappear into a world that would destroy her.

When he made it back to the exam room, it was to find Perci holding the little girl tightly, while the mother paced around the room, demanding answers about when she could take her daughter home. Never once did the mother move to touch her frightened daughter. Her entire focus was on Perci—her current enemy.

The words that woman was spewing at Perci were the kind no child should ever have to hear.

Perci was silent, for once. But when she looked up and her Tyler blue eyes met his, he saw the relief. "Mrs. North, Ivy will be going to an approved foster home when she's discharged."

He braced himself for the barrage that the child's mother threw at him.

It didn't end until Joel arrived and took the woman away in handcuffs. On assault charges. And charges of child abuse—her husband had left her two months earlier and died in a car accident in Montana a week after that. He'd plowed his truck into a semi-trailer after a night of excessive partying. At the time, his blood alcohol limit had been more than twice the legal amount.

It had been the mother who had hurt little Ivy this time.

No more. Nate was prepared to call in every favor he could to see that this little one stayed safe from now on.

PERCI WAITED UNTIL HER BROTHER-IN-LAW led Mrs. North away from the exam room in cuffs before finally letting go of Ivy. The little girl had become nearly hysterical the instant her mother had raised her voice. Perci probably had child-sized claw marks in her shoulders. Ivy hadn't wanted to let Perci go.

And the mother had come at them both. With claws extended.

All Perci had been able to do was wrap her arms around the little girl and twist away from the much larger woman. She'd protected as much as she had been able to.

Nate had been there. Nate and Joel. They'd jumped in front of her and Ivy without hesitation. Protecting her. And the child who had had no one else.

She looked up at Nate, gaze landing on the red scratch on his cheek. She tucked a blanket around the little girl, then grabbed a package of gauze off the counter. And antiseptic. Human nails held a variety of bacteria. He couldn't afford for it to get infected.

The red mark on Nate's cheek ticked her off more than she ever would have thought possible.

She pressed the gauze against his cheek gently. "What happens now?"

His face tightened even more. "Get her things together."

Perci looked at the child. She was so alone. Perci had always had her family to count on. Little Ivy didn't even have that. "Where is she going, though?"

"With me."

"What?"

"Levi and I are licensed by the state. For teenagers. It was the best anyone could do with the floods—and the shortage of foster parents in this part of the state. The other option was a group home."

Perci shook her head immediately. The very idea horrified her. "No. She can't...she'll be alone."

"So she's coming home with me. Well, to your sister, anyway. Pan will be the primary caregiver during the days."

"Pan's not there. Neither is Levi. Pan called. Rowland needed her in Hollywood to reshoot a half-dozen scenes. She and Levi flew out four hours ago. I spoke with her on my break."

"Then I guess Ivy's coming home with *me*." He winced, whether from the antiseptic on his cheek or the idea of what was happening to Ivy. "I'm not sure how she'll handle that."

The little girl was so frightened of men in general—it would be literal hell for Ivy to wake up with only a strange man around. Especially one who had just argued with her mother. Afraid, hurting, alone. The little girl would just not understand.

But Ivy knew Perci. She'd been the nurse on duty the last three times the little girl had been brought in. And she had stayed with the little girl all three times. Perci wasn't her mother or her family, but it would be better for Ivy. "I'll come with you. She'll...need me."

That little girl *needed* her, and Perci wasn't going to abandon her now. Not with Ivy already being so alone.

9

One of the other nurses on shift provided a car seat. Everyone knew of little Ivy North—it had been a matter of time until Social Services acted on the child's behalf. They had all just been waiting. Before Perci and Nate left for the evening, another nurse ran to her own home three blocks over and grabbed a bag of clothing her twin daughter and son had outgrown. Some of the clothing would be boys', but she doubted Ivy would mind.

Everything else, either Nate would already have in his own home, or would be available at Perci's. Ivy would be set for a few days, anyway.

Until more permanent arrangements could be made.

Perci removed the hospital gown and quickly dressed Ivy in clean, dry clothes, and a small rain jacket. She brushed the girl's blond curls while she waited for Nate to text that he had his truck ready. Ivy just sat and stared. Her eyes would dart to the door, as if waiting for her mother to reappear. But she never asked where her mother was.

Perci's heart broke over and over with each look of anxiety, of fear, of worry, that crossed the little face.

No two-year-old should ever live in such utter terror.

No matter what happened, Perci was going to do her best to ensure that Ivy had a good future. One with people who loved her.

Like Perci had been loved.

Her family hadn't had much monetarily, but they had had love. Her parents had never struck her or her siblings. Not even once. It had gotten tight on them so many times, food had even been scarce a time or two, but they had protected one another. Loved one another.

Nate texted.

Perci scooped Ivy up and grabbed her own

bag. "Let's go find Dr. Nate, sweetie. He'll take us...home."

It wasn't their home. Either of them. But she was going to make it the best place for Ivy that she could. Ivy fought getting in the car with Nate. Perci ended up in the backseat, doing her best to soothe. Until the girl fell asleep.

When they pulled into Nate's front drive, the rains had doubled, lightning flashed everywhere, and thunder was so loud she could barely think.

Ivy slept on.

Nate lifted the child from the car, and Perci covered her with a blanket quickly. Then it was a mad dash to the front door for all of them.

He settled Ivy in the center of the queen bed in the guest room and pulled another quilt over her. "The pain medicine should keep her sedated for the rest of the night."

"Poor kid. What's going to happen to her? After all of this? Her mother will eventually get out of jail. Does she just go right back to her?"

"No. I don't think she's going back to her mother. Not anytime soon." Nate slipped his fingers around her elbow and guided her out of the guest room, like she was helpless or something.

Perci would have protested—at any other time. But this time she didn't.

The entire situation was making her feel beyond vulnerable.

Like it or not, she and Nate were in this together.

Them and a little girl who had no one else.

10

Nate was up first. He immediately made breakfast for the two females still sleeping in his guest room. He didn't know what else to do. It was his—and Perci's—day off from the hospital. He could focus on finding a better solution somehow. He wasn't equipped to care for a toddler long term, and his early morning phone call to his brother Levi had made it clear that that was exactly what it was going to be. Levi expected to be in Hollywood for at least two weeks.

There was no way he could shift his life around to account for a traumatized child for that long, not while running an entire damned hospital.

At least...not without help.

That left him two options—ask his mother for help. Or convince Perci that *she* wanted to stay right where she was and help him care for Ivy.

He could get his sister-in-law Phoebe to care for Ivy while he and Perci worked. But at night, when it was just him and Ivy rattling around in the ranch house, he wanted Perci there.

They had brought Ivy here together; they would help Ivy here together. Period.

Perci wandered into the kitchen, wearing sweats he'd seen on Pan a dozen times now, and carrying Ivy on her hip. The child's eyes were red. The bruises on her arm stood out. She clung to Perci like the woman was the only safety she had in the world.

He'd always had a soft spot for kids. "Hey, Ivy-bear. Are you hungry?" He'd made her oatmeal, with a touch of brown sugar. It had always been Levi's favorite as a kid. Oatmeal and fruit had been Joel's. Nate had sliced her some strawberries to go with the oatmeal.

Perci chattered at Ivy, doing what she could to calm the child down. It wasn't easy. Finally, Perci had her in the chair on a thick cushion, while Perci spoon fed her the oatmeal.

Ivy continued to eye him like he was the monster under her bed.

But finally, after only the strawberries remained, Ivy smiled.

Nate's own lips stretched into a smile.

The child's smile was *almost* as powerful as the woman's next to her. And he was a total goner.

IT WAS HARD TO DESPISE A MAN WHO WENT TO so much trouble to make a frightened child smile. Perci couldn't keep her guard up between them like this. He just looked so much better than perfect, wiping Ivy's cheeks gently.

She had no idea what she was going to do with him.

He hadn't only made breakfast for Ivy—he'd made a bowl for himself and Perci, as well. They sat together, eating and saying very little, while Ivy babbled at her. The little girl still shot nervous looks at Nate, but she was calming toward him slightly.

It would take a little more time before she was completely comfortable with him.

Of course, Ivy wasn't *her* responsibility. She was Nate's. Completely.

Perci should be heading out, doing her own things. She didn't want to. She wanted to stay right where she was.

Perci didn't think it was only because of Ivy. Something had changed.

She didn't know what it was. It might have been the way he'd been so willing to fight for the child that had mattered most. He hadn't been going to give in until Ivy had been safe.

When it had looked iffy, Perci had instinctively looked to *him* instead of Joel to make everything all right. To just *fix* everything. Long after she'd crawled into the bed in the room next to the sleeping little girl's, she'd thought about exactly that.

Thought about what it meant. She still didn't have a clue what to do about him.

"Stay."

Perci stared at him over the table. "Excuse me?"

"Stay. Here. Help me with her. Make sure I don't screw this up."

"I can't do that." She wanted to. She didn't want to leave Ivy, for one thing. For another, it felt right exactly where she was. "I have...things to do."

A lame excuse and they both knew it. "Persephone..."

"Don't." She held up her free hand. "I can't stay here. The two of us will argue. Right in front of her. And terrify her all over again. For another... I just can't. I have my own life at the ranch and the hospital. I just can't abandon that to hang around Masterson-ville."

He stood, looking long and tall and so damned strong her breath caught. Then he was at her side of the table, squatting down next to her and Ivy. "Stay. *Help* me. Levi will be back within two weeks. Then Pan can help. She's already said she would. Just...stay. We'll take her to Phoebe while we work. But I think she needs *you* right now. Far more than she needs me. She needs to see that not all women are like her mother."

"Then I'll take her with me." But that wouldn't work. He had to be the primary caregiver until Levi returned. She had an idea how it was all working out. In order for Levi to have become a foster parent, everyone in his house had had to be vetted. Checked out and approved. That meant Nate.

Not her.

Ivy shoved another strawberry into her mouth. Perci watched her for a moment. Ivy was so vulnerable.

Perci knew what it was like to be at the mercy of someone else. She couldn't do it—she could not leave the little girl, even though she knew without a doubt that Nate would never do anything to hurt Ivy.

"Fine. But I need to run to the grocery store for the kids and my dad, and to get some of my things."

"Then that's what we'll do today. And we can get her some more kid-friendly food. Pan usually does the shopping, but since she's gone, I'm not sure what we have that Ivy will eat."

"Kids eat the same thing that adults eat. Mostly. You'll need easier snack foods and quicker lunches. Healthy ones." Perci's mind was already running over the types of meals they prepared for their younger brothers. And a mental list of everything else Ivy might need. "Can we make it to town? Are the floods bad, you think?"

"I spoke with Joel. Roads between here and your dad's place and town are all clear." He scooped Ivy up. The little girl squeaked, but didn't cry this time. It was an improvement. Ivy looked so small against Nate's muscled chest. "Let's get going. We'll get your things first, talk to Phoebe, and then get to the market before the rains start up again."

Perci had no choice but to nod. It seemed like there was nothing she could do to resist. He was luring her in. Trapping her in his world. Just like she'd always known he would the instant she became vulnerable again.

And just like her namesake, she felt helpless to resist.

11

Phoebe greeted her with a wide-eyed expression that asked its own questions. Perci just shook her head. She and her older sister would talk —later. When she didn't have Nate and Ivy hanging on her every word. The car ride hadn't started out too well, but Perci had made a point of reassuring Ivy that she could sit in the backseat without Perci right next to her.

Perci gave Phoebe a scaled-down version of events and told her older sister where she'd be staying until Pan returned and could take official custody of Ivy.

Phoebe's eyes held a knowing smirk that irritated her beyond measure. But Perci said nothing in return. Phoebe agreed to watch Ivy when Nate and Perci returned to work—Phoebe would have the three boys around to help entertain Ivy. They still had two days to get through.

With her and Nate playing Mommy and Daddy.

What she had agreed to do was completely crazy, but when Ivy wrapped little arms around her neck and refused to go to her sister, Perci understood exactly why she had agreed to do it.

For Ivy. And maybe for herself, too. She needed to help Ivy, needed to make a difference again.

Nate waited on the porch, speaking quietly with Perci's father.

Her dad had always liked and respected all of the Masterson brothers—even with the trouble that had existed between Nate and Perci. Nate stepped back inside, to talk to Phoebe about details, leaving her alone with her father. Her father patted Ivy on the back lightly, then kissed Perci's forehead. "You call me, baby girl, if you need me."

"I will, Daddy."

"Good. We'll be here...when you come home." There was a look in his eyes that had her pausing. Wondering.

"Daddy?"

"Yes?" He cupped her cheek gently and just stared.

"What's wrong?"

He smiled. "Not a damned thing. I'm just thinking of how absolutely proud I am of you. What you've accomplished in just a few years— any father would be proud to have you as his daughter. Your mother's probably smiling down on you now."

"I miss her." Perci would never forget the terror from the night her mother had been hurt, the pain that had consumed her after her mother had died three days later. The way no one had *believed* her when she'd said it hadn't been her brother's fault, but the fault of the other driver.

The fear and harassment and anxiety that had been her constant companion ever since.

Now that was coming to light. Joel coming into their lives had changed everything.

But it was a little too late. The damage had long been done.

"I know. Some days it's far worse than others." Her mother would have known exactly what to do with the little girl now napping on her shoulder. And would have fought to do it, if need be. Perci always remembered her mother when it was time to fight. There wasn't anything her mother wouldn't have done for one of her children. "My arm's going numb."

"You look good with a child, sweetie. Natural. More than your sisters, you have a way with the little ones. Maybe someday it'll be you giving me a grandchild like your sister."

"I get it. Pip is going to be the favorite for a while." All of her sisters would be having children of their own soon. Moving on to the next stage in their lives.

Perci wouldn't. Not yet.

She hadn't yet found the man she trusted enough to even want to think about doing something so life-changing with. *When* she finally decided to be in love with someone, trust would come first. A long time before anything else.

Trust. Safety. It would be easy with that man. She'd feel exactly like she belonged.

Nate stepped back outside. Perci looked up at him just as he smiled.

At her.

When was the last time he'd smiled *at her* just like that? She honestly couldn't remember.

They had fought for so long.

She felt strange, vulnerable. Tender. Not *for* him, but like she'd been kicked or bruised and was just learning to deal with it.

Hell of a way to feel about a man. Like a mule had kicked her in the chest and she wasn't certain if something was broken or not.

"You ready?" he asked, holding out her jacket to her. She'd grabbed it from her room a few minutes earlier and tossed it over the back of her chair at the table. She nodded.

He held the jacket open for her and helped her slip it on around the sleeping child.

It might have been her imagination, but she was almost certain Nate's hands lingered.

Touched her just a little more than she was ready to think about.

12

His wife's boy had thrown him off his property. Told him that he had no business showing up the way he had. Clive still smarted at that. He had raised that boy as if he were his own son, and Clint treated him no better than shit.

Hell, Clive didn't even know why he'd bothered going out there. The baby and Clint really weren't his business.

But they *were* all he had left. Maria had been right in that. He'd never have grandchildren of his own flesh. That hope had died with Jay. It would take him a while to get past that.

But Clint...Clint was second best. He'd been

raised right. He was making a good showing with the Wyoming State Police and was doing his best to get that ranch running that he'd inherited from his mother's parents.

All while trying to raise that baby girl on his own.

Any man would be proud to call Clint his son. But Clive? Clive just didn't have it in him to give a shit any more.

Not since Jay.

Everything he had done for the past thirty years had been for *Jay.*

And all of that was gone.

Clive wandered around the town's only market aimlessly. He couldn't remember why he'd come inside in the first place. He supposed he ought to buy something, a man needed to eat, and all.

The woman who owned the place was a skinny blonde around Jay's age. He didn't know much about her. He would have, at one point. She'd moved to Masterson well after Clive had lost his bid for sheriff this last time.

To a damned *Masterson.*

Mastersons had cost him everything.

His life's work. His only son. His self-respect.

Everything.

He rounded the aisle and came face-to-face with one of those sonsofbitches. A redheaded woman walked at his side.

Another one of those damned Tylers.

He studied her for a moment, wondering if it was this one who had gotten his son killed.

He didn't think it was. That one worked the ranch and dressed like exactly what she was. And was usually with her husband, the vet.

This twin didn't wear a wedding ring. The big brute at her side was the doctor, not the veterinarian. Or so he thought. Clive wasn't entirely certain which Tyler twin was which—or which Masterson doctor was which, for that matter. Other than the new sheriff, he didn't know the Mastersons at all. The way they'd all intermarried, it left a person even more confused.

Those Mastersons had had everything they'd ever wanted.

His boy had lost everything, including his own life, for one of those damned Tyler girls.

"*Masterson.*" His words were for the man, but his eyes...his eyes wouldn't leave the woman. He knew who she was now.

Perci. He and Perci...well...of all the Tyler girls, he knew *this* one the best.

Tyler blue eyes widened when they looked at him.

The child in her arms barely registered with Clive at all.

13

NATE'S HAND LANDED ON PERCI'S SHOULDER before he even realized he had moved. With a simple nudge, he had Perci and Ivy tucked closer to his side. Protected.

He didn't like the light in Clive Gunderson's eyes. The way the man stared at Perci was almost fanatical.

With hatred.

Gunderson was making it very clear for anyone within viewing distance that he could not stand Perci. Or Nate.

But the situation was Gunderson's own fault.

He'd heard the story of Sheriff Gunderson

straight from his youngest sister-in-law's own mouth. She had had nothing good to say about the Gundersons. No Tyler had.

Pan had told them exactly how often and what kind of hell Clive Gunderson had put her and her sisters through. To hide what his son Jay had tried to do to Pip.

Pan had hinted that Perci had suffered most of all. That Gunderson would follow Perci home from classes and pull her over. On an almost-monthly basis. To remind them all to keep their mouths shut.

The harassments had been beyond horrific.

No one knew exactly what had happened to Perci out there alone on the road with Clive Gunderson. Perci had never told her sisters what he'd done to her. Pan had said she'd refused to talk about what that man had done. That she was terrified every time the man's name was mentioned.

His fist tightened with the urge to ram it into Gunderson's face. Show that sonofabitch that she was no longer vulnerable. That she had him, and all of his brothers, to stop assholes like Gunderson from ever getting near her again.

Instead, he spread his fingers wide over her

back, then slid them up to cup her narrow shoulder.

"Gunderson." He wasn't going to say he was sorry for Clive Gunderson's loss. Maybe he should be—he was a doctor, after all. He had taken an oath to heal.

Jay Gunderson had almost killed three people Nate loved. That would never be forgotten.

His hand tightened on Perci's shoulder, almost involuntarily. She looked up at him, a question in her Tyler blue eyes. He shook his head minutely, then guided her and the grocery cart—and Ivy, who was clinging to her—around the man half blocking the aisle.

"I hope you know what you have, Masterson. It sure as hell burns when you lose it." Gunderson's tone was guttural, broken.

Menacing.

Nate turned back to the man, making certain he was between Gunderson and Perci and Ivy, just in case the man snapped. "You planning on making trouble, Gunderson? I don't think that would be a smart idea."

"Nate..." Perci slipped in front of him and turned. Her hand rose, landed in the exact center of his chest. Hell, it was probably all that stopped him from making a scene. "Don't. Not here...Ivy..."

FOR ONE HALF SECOND, SHE WAS ALMOST certain Nate was going to charge Gunderson right there in the midst of the IGA. His hand covered hers, and he squeezed, without even looking down at her. Big, strong, protective.

She shivered.

It was rather hard to be afraid of Gunderson when a man like Nate was right there.

She trusted him. To keep her safe, to protect Ivy, and to just...make everything ok.

That thought completely rocked her off her foundation.

She *trusted* Nate Masterson.

Perci tried to tell herself it was the same as the way she trusted his brothers, but she knew it was a lie. She hadn't ever been great at deluding herself. Everything about Nate was different from his brothers.

Gunderson stared at them as they walked away. She could almost feel a knife in her back from his gaze. Nate leaned down after they'd rounded the corner. "Don't ever let him see you're afraid. Gunderson's a damned snake. The whole lot of them are."

She nodded. "You don't need to tell *me* that."

Clive Gunderson had gloated when her mother had died. Had said the Tylers always got what they deserved. She would never be able to forget that. Or forgive. He could have helped them more that night. But he hadn't. She'd always wondered if her mother had died partially because of *his* neglect. But that was an answer she'd never get. And all those nights when he'd been waiting for her alongside the highway...she would *never* forget that fear. She never knew when he'd be out there. Sometimes he'd pull her over and hold her alongside the road for hours. She'd always told her family she'd worked late at the ER whenever it happened. She shivered again. She would never forget the nights she'd end up sneaking in to her room and cry from anger and frustration and terror. Because of Clive Gunderson. "Let's just get what we need and get out of here. Forget about him. Please?"

He nodded.

And kept his hand on her. For once, Perci didn't mind.

Ivy had sensed the tension that had risen and had started fussing a bit. Perci cuddled her for a long moment. Nate moved closer still, almost surrounding them with his much bigger body.

Protecting them from the rest of the world around them.

14

RHEA KNEW SOMETHING WAS *UP* WITH ONE OF her boys. A mother always did. Since Levi was in Hollywood, of all places, she'd passed Joel driving the squad truck on her way into town, and Matt was right there in the diner with that sweet little wife of his, that left only one option.

Nate. She sighed. Of course. It had always been Nate who had given her trouble. From the time her third son had made his somewhat difficult appearance in this world, he'd been fighting everything.

He should have married that girl months ago. It took Rhea some checking with her sources—social media was great for meddling mothers, which was exactly what she aspired to be. Before she found out something that shocked her.

But it also gave her hope. And a little bit of a tender feeling inside to know her boy was going above and beyond to do the right thing.

She had raised him right, contrary, though, he could be.

She just had to swing by and see how the two were getting along—and check on that precious little one for herself.

Nate's truck was parked in front of the house he shared with his brother. Rhea didn't bother knocking, but she made certain to be quiet in case the child was sleeping.

She was. Curled up on the couch with another chair pushed up like a rail and a quilt Rhea's own mother had made when the boys were babies. Rhea studied the toddler for a moment, first as a doctor, and then as a temporary grandmama. There were bruises that would never belong there, but they would heal. The girl looked like a little angel right there. Rhea's heart melted.

Her arms ached to hold. As soon as that little one woke, she'd be doing exactly that.

Perci slept curled up in a big recliner nearby. Nate worked at the table in the kitchen. Rhea studied him for a long moment, that rush of motherly pride no longer shocking her when she looked at the boys she'd raised.

Nate had always done her and his father proud.

He was the one who looked the most like and acted the most like his father, and had grown to be as big as his father, too. She missed that man every single day. Nate was a living look into the past, though he had her eyes and hair.

The pain was finally starting to not stab through her, though. The love she and her husband shared had been deep and lasting.

She wanted the same thing for her sons. Three had that.

This stubborn holdout was being ridiculous. He really was just like his father. Daniel had fought her like wildfire all those years ago, too. He'd said she was too young, had too much of a future ahead of her with med school, and hadn't needed to get distracted by *him*.

Fooey on that. She'd seduced him the first month she'd known him. Six months later, they had been expecting Joel, and she'd been about to enter med school—and they'd been married two months. A year after Joel had come Matt. Fourteen months after that had been Nate. Twenty months after Nate had come Levi.

Her boys.

"Well, there you are. Heard about the excitement."

"Mom, have you eaten lunch?" He barely reacted to her comment, just giving her that dark look his father had perfected long before this version of him had been born. Rhea smirked. She'd had decades of experience dealing with that look. Nate didn't stand a chance.

"Not yet."

He grabbed her a bowl and spooned out some soup from the pot on the stove. "Pan froze some soup when she was here last. That girl can cook."

"I'd like to meet her again. The last time I saw her she was covered in amniotic fluid." She'd delivered all three of her daughters-in-law. Beautiful babies, the lot of them. The twins had been a difficult birth, but their mother had pulled through. And gone on to have a bunch more. Unfortunately, they'd switched physicians after Pan's birth, to one closer to their ranch.

Rhea hadn't thought of that particular branch of the Tylers in years until she'd hired Perci.

"You will. As soon as Rowland Bowles is finished with her."

"I can't imagine seeing three of my daughters-in-law and my own son in a movie. I'm sorry I missed it." There was a lot she'd missed.

Grief had been what had mostly sent her running. Everywhere she'd turned, she'd seen her husband. To the point where she hadn't wanted to look at the boys they'd created together.

She'd had to get away before she lost herself. Leaving so Nate could find his way was just her convenient excuse. Rhea had had to find her purpose in life without Daniel. She had made a difference out there, helping those in need.

She was back now. It was time to move on to the next stage in life. Grandmother-hood. And there was a little one starting to fuss in the living room that she could start with. She knew Ivy North's history—and she'd call in every favor she could to ensure that child remained safe.

Right where she was.

Nate stood. "I'd better get her before she wakes Perci. I don't think either of them slept well."

Nate would have known if that girl had been

in his bed where she belonged. Rhea bit back a sigh.

He was as stubborn as his father.

She'd had to seduce Nate's father thirty-eight years ago, too.

Maybe she needed to give Perci some pointers. That girl really needed to pick up the pace. It was best to just blitz Nate. Not let him know what's hit him. Otherwise, her son would snail-pace everything to death.

Just like his father.

Her other three took after her in that regard: when they knew what they wanted, they went with it. But Nate? Nate had to analyze and ponder everything to the nth degree.

Infuriating.

A tear touched her eye. Damn it, she really missed him. Daniel would be so proud of those boys they'd raised. Just like she was. The fifteen months she'd been without him had seemed like a lifetime.

15

NATE READJUSTED THE BLANKET OVER PERCI and then scooped up the now awake Ivy. She fussed a bit, but didn't resist him holding her.

Ivy wanted Perci; it was obvious in the way the little girl looked at the woman in the chair and fussed. "Shhh. Let Perci sleep. She's sleepy."

"Perci's napping, but Ivy is very hungry." Big eyes blinked at him sadly. "Very hungry."

"Then we'll feed you." He held her close and rocked. He'd checked her bruises himself that morning. She'd be due for some pain medication soon, but she was making good progress. The best thing for her was to rest and heal. To know she was in a safe place. "There's ice cream, if you eat your soup first."

His mother was still in the kitchen, but had pulled vegetables from the fridge. "There's a roast in the freezer that hasn't frozen yet and still enough time to make it. I'll throw it in. That way you and Perci don't have to worry about dinner. How long do you expect to have the little princess?"

"I don't know. Levi's technically the foster parent on record at this point. And it all depends on how things resolve with her mother. It was her third offense. If the charges stick, then she'll be facing a minimum of five years in Wyoming. There were other charges outstanding from Montana." Joel had called him that morning for an update on Ivy, first. And to let Nate know that her mother was going away for a long while. "And Colorado. She has a history."

"So Ivy's future is unsettled." His mother shot him a pointed look. "How long do you plan to keep that girl in *there*?"

"As long as she's needed." Today had been a surprisingly calm day so far. He and Perci had focused on playing and snuggling Ivy. They'd even curled up on the couch before the nap and watched a children's movie Perci's brothers had left behind. Before he'd known it, Perci's head had landed on his shoulder and then Ivy's on his chest.

It had felt so damned *right* he hadn't wanted to even think about moving.

So he hadn't.

For a very long time.

It had given him a lot to think about.

Maybe he should just *give* in. Go after what was right there in front of him. Fall in line with everyone's expectations.

It wouldn't be a restful kind of life with Perci Tyler, but it might very well be worth it. They'd no doubt argue, but the times in between would be... wonderful. Passionate. Perci did everything with passion.

"Were you and Dad always happy?" The question popped out before he could stop it. His parents had one of the fieriest and most passionate marriages he'd ever seen.

"Always? No. Mostly—hell, yes, we were *mostly* happy. He just made my world brighter, Nathaniel. In a way you can't ever understand until you feel that same kind of love. It's different than the love you feel for your brothers, or your parents, or even your child. Why do you ask?"

"Just thinking. About Joel, Matt, and Levi. About their wives. Pan and Levi remind me of you and Dad."

"Any particular reason?"

He shot his mother a look. "Don't be difficult."

She smiled, an expression very much like Levi's most wicked. "What did I say?"

"I was just wondering."

"Of course, you were. Perci's staying until Ivy's situation is figured out."

"And just how quickly do you see that happening?"

Nate hesitated. They both were old enough to know that there was no easy answer to that question. And that Perci would have to go home, eventually. "I don't honestly know. She could be here for quite a while."

"Then you'll need to figure out what to do next, won't you?"

16

HE JUST COULDN'T STAY AWAY. CLIVE HAD found himself following the girl and that damned Masterson when they'd left the market. They had a kid with them. A girl he didn't recognize. Had to be one of those damned Tylers, though.

Nothing but a bunch of trouble, *that* family. They always had been.

Clive had had more than his fair share of trouble with the Tylers.

Masterson took her inside. She had the kid on her hip. They looked perfect, damn them. Their lives were going to go so damned smooth, while he had to spend the rest of his grieving his boy.

It wasn't right.

Clive stayed on the outskirts of that Masterson property, just thinking. Remembering. He remembered every interaction he'd had with any of those Tyler girls, starting with the night Jay had gotten too carried away over that quieter twin.

That was the night that had changed everything. Clive should have handled it differently. Maybe if *he* had treated those girls a bit better, they would have been willing to help his son more when Jay had needed it most.

But it wasn't *Clive's* fault. It wasn't. And what he'd done those nights alongside the road had been to protect Jay. To protect *his son*.

He thought about going back to town, to that vet's office, and finding *her*.

Seeing what was so special about her that his son had died because of it.

But he didn't.

Not because he was a coward or anything. But that husband of hers would just complicate things in a way Clive didn't want to mess with now.

He knew Perci better. She would be the one most likely to give him the answers he needed. If he decided to ask those questions. He had enough experience with her to know just how to scare the shit out of her, if he needed to.

And she'd leave that doctor eventually, anyway. She wouldn't have that Masterson around to protect her forever.

Clive *could* ask her exactly what was burning in his head.

If he wanted to.

Clive wasn't certain that he did. It didn't matter, after all. What was done was done.

Jay was dead.

Nothing Clive did was going to change that.

17

Ivy didn't want her to leave, but Phoebe was good at getting children to trust her. Her sister always had been. When Phoebe and Joel finally had children of their own, Perci's nieces or nephews would be extremely lucky. Just like Perci and her own siblings had been. Phoebe was very much like Perci's mother had been.

Still, leaving Ivy when she'd been crying like that had been harder than Perci would have ever expected. She'd felt like she'd abandoned the little girl.

Which was ridiculous.

Phoebe was probably going to be better at dealing with Ivy than Perci ever would be.

Her immediate supervisor was waiting when she walked in. "There you are. Heard you had some serious excitement a few days ago. How's little Ivy doing?"

Perci smiled, but knew it wasn't a good one. Visions of Ivy crying for her the entire day kept running through Perci's head. "She's doing ok. She had a tough time when I left her with my sister, but...I can't take any more time off right now. Not if I want my brothers to be able to eat."

Tiff patted her on the shoulder. "I know. It gets easier with time. Leaving your little ones behind. Every working mother goes through it."

"But I'm not her mother. I'm just...babysitting her for now."

"That's what you say *now*. How's Dr. Nate doing with her? I can't say I ever thought he'd be the one to take a child home like this. But then again, maybe I do. There's a goodness in that man."

"Hmmm. I suppose." What was she supposed to say to that? Everyone in the hospital knew how she and Nate felt about each other. But how she felt about that man had changed drastically over the past two days. Seeing him with Ivy, as gentle as he'd been...and the way he'd looked at *her* when Perci would least expect it...

"Where is he?"

Tiff grinned. "In his office. His *mother* is here. Giving him fits again. Apparently she wants to start working here again. In *our* department."

Perci hid a wince. Rhea had been there yesterday afternoon when Perci had woken from her nap. "I see."

"You're working the ER today. We had to do some switching around. Jackie's kids both have the flu. And T.J.'s car wouldn't start. Supposedly."

"Gotcha." Routine would help. Get her right back to where she was supposed to be. No more playing house with Ivy and Nate Masterson.

At least for a little while.

Perci closed her eyes when Tiff stepped away, and pulled in a deep breath. She resisted the urge to text Phoebe again to check on Ivy.

It would be best just to get everything back to normal again.

Somehow. As soon as this was finished with Ivy, she had her own family to take care of. Responsibilities that would not wait forever.

Her dad needed her to do just that. The boys

needed her to do just that, too. She couldn't...be distracted by Nate Masterson and Ivy forever.

She just couldn't.

18

HE HADN'T WANTED TO COME TO THE ER. NOT the Masterson County one, anyway. But Clive knew that if he'd made too big of a fuss, Maria would figure it out. And he didn't need the questions.

As luck would have it, the Tyler girl was working the ER when he was wheeled in. The scratch on his leg wasn't too bad, but there was no way in hell he wanted *her* touching him. He pulled on Maria's sleeve. "Get me another nurse. I don't want that Tyler woman near me."

Maria's surprise was written in her big, dark eyes. Then they cleared, as if she understood. "Of course, honey."

The hospital ER wasn't big, and it was curtained off for exam bays. It needed a good updating, but he had to admit the man running the hospital was doing a damned fine job of it.

Except with Jay.

No doubt that Masterson doctor had deliberately left his boy to die like that. Revenge. For that girl. That twin to this one. They'd both been there; had probably seized the opportunity to get back at Clive for all those nights on the highway. "Damned bitch."

"Clive!" Maria's tone held her surprise, and no wonder. Clive did his best not to ever curse in front of her. Maria was old-fashioned like that. It had taken him over a year just to get her clothes off.

"It's the truth. Damned Tylers are the reason my boy is dead. I'll never forget that."

"Are they? *Jay* went after her sister, Clive. No sense lying to yourself about it. What happened was a tragedy. No doubt. But not one those sweet girls caused. Everyone knows that. Let's get your leg taken care of."

He sat there and seethed.

Even Maria believed the lies then.

He'd never felt so damned alone in his life.

That didn't change when Maria called Clint to come get him so she could go on in to work at that bookstore in town. The one owned by that cousin of the Tylers.

Tylers were just everywhere now.

It sure shocked the hell out of him when that boy showed up to do just that.

The boy wheeled him out to the old ranch truck Clint had driven for years and told Clive to stay put. Clint wasn't happy about picking him up, no doubt.

Clive supposed he should be thankful Clint was there at all. "Where's the baby?"

"With the new...housekeeper."

"Finally got someone out there?" Rumor was his wife's boy had been having some trouble getting a woman to stay out there in that heap of a ranch house, caring for that baby of his. Hell, he couldn't blame them. That place needed some serious work. Work Clint couldn't afford.

He doubted Clint was paying the housekeeper even a living wage, considering what Clint made with the highway patrol.

What kind of help could Clint get for that baby with no damned money to pay for it? Probably not good, that was what.

Clive winced. He could help the boy out with some cash, he supposed.

He had nothing else to do with the small amount of savings he'd built over the years.

It had been intended for Jay someday. When his boy had been mature enough to deserve it.

He supposed giving it to his stepson for Paula's grandbaby was good enough as any reason. She'd have wanted the best for that girl.

He'd call his lawyer in the morning. Have it taken care of. If nothing else, he'd set it up in an account for that baby.

Clint hesitated. "I got a new woman out there now. I'm not sure she'll work out. Let's get you home. I don't like leaving Violet with a stranger if I can help it."

"Don't coddle her." He had Jay, and he knew it. Maybe if he had been as tough on Jay as he had been on Clint, things would have turned out differently. "Make her tough. So she can survive in this world better than your brother did."

"Don't worry about it. I'll make sure Violet survives just fine. In my own way."

Clive did what the boy told him to do, when Clint went back inside to retrieve Clive's wallet and belt he'd left inside. He should have done it

earlier, gotten his things himself, but Clive had insisted the boy get him away from that Tyler girl and
that Masterson boyfriend of hers—who had stood
in the midst of that damned hospital and glowered
right at him. Big-ass brute, that was for sure.

That Masterson had it out for him, and Clive
knew it.

Probably because of that girl who had been
nothing but trouble for Clive for the last three
years.

Her car was right there. Next to Clint's truck.

Clive had no trouble recognizing it. He'd
watched for it weekly for years.

Whenever he'd been bored out there as sheriff
and out late for whatever reason, he'd go find her.
Have a little fun. Just to keep his skills sharp. He'd
only ticketed her twice, but he must have pulled
her over dozens of times. There at the end, she'd
not say a word to him. Just look at him with those
blue eyes of hers. Not fighting. Just freezing him
out. Taking it.

So he'd leave the rest of her family alone.

It had been like a little secret deal the two of
them had had going between them for all that
time.

Yes, he'd known Perci Tyler for *years*.

Since that night Jay had first done something stupid with that Tyler girl and changed everything.

Hell, half of his entertainment had come from pulling that nurse over, first when she was a student, and then after. Just to remind her that *he* could still make trouble for her.

That had ended when he'd retired to work his ranch after losing the election to that damned Joel Masterson a little over a year and a half ago.

Mastersons.

Those bastards had ruined everything. Taken *everything* from him. And now Masterson was getting that pretty girl, just like his brother had gotten the twin Jay had wanted.

Everything was ruined.

He hadn't felt so damned impotent in a long damned time.

Clive pushed the wheelchair toward the rear of the car. It took him only seconds to pour the contents of the extra-large coffee Maria had bought him down the gas tank of that little car.

It would cause some damage. No doubt about that. He amused himself for a moment, imagining the little car going over the shoulder at Wreck Road Curve, just like her mama's had.

It still left him feeling about as useless as teats on a warthog. Completely without purpose for the rest of his life.

19

———

NATE DIDN'T GET ON HER CASE EVEN ONCE. HE almost seemed to be avoiding her. Until he came out of his office about five minutes before she was to clock out, his mother at his side. The look of exhaustion on his face told its own story.

And the irritation.

She felt for him in that moment. His mother still terrified her. Tiff had told her the older woman had been in Nate's office most of the day. Going over his files. Questioning.

Nate wouldn't have liked that, even if it was by his mother. She suspected it was *because* it was his mother.

He called her over, then leaned down to

whisper in her ear. "I'm going to be here for a few more hours, I think. Unless you can come up with something to get me out of her clutches. I'll give you everything I own including my soul, if you will. Including my ranch."

"Trying to trick me, Masterson?" Her words lacked the heat they would have even a week ago. Now she just felt...compassion. He just looked beyond exhausted.

"Something like that."

"I'm going to head out to get Ivy. I'm sure she's ok, Phoebe texted that she was, but I don't want to leave her for too long today. Not the first day." After what had happened with Phoebe and Joel, Joel had insisted they all start carrying cell phones. They'd found the money with help from their father's business partner in Texas. The man had invested in their ranch, and it had been the boost they'd needed. He was shipping his own particular brand of feed up from his ranch in Texas. It had saved them enough to afford a few luxuries, like cell phones and better internet than what they'd had before.

Perci no longer had to work sixty hour weeks, unless she wanted to.

"Call me when you get home...back to my house, I mean."

"I will."

He surprised her when he tugged her jacket up over her shoulders a bit straighter. "Be careful. I'll see you and Ivy when I get home, sweetheart."

His volume had dropped, become intimate. Just for her. She looked into his green eyes and just *knew* the man was temptation in itself.

If she wasn't careful, he was going to change everything.

Perci clocked out and hurried across the parking lot. It had started to rain an hour ago. The jacket Nate had adjusted was waterproof. She shouldn't get *too* wet. She'd get to her father's place, get Ivy, then head home.

She'd made it halfway to her car before what she'd thought had sunken in. Her *home*. Her home was with her father, not *Nate Masterson*. What had the man done, tricked her or something?

No. It had to be because of Ivy. Nothing else made sense.

She cursed slightly when she saw the door over her gas tank had flopped open again. She needed to get that fixed somehow.

It seemed like she had spent all of her spare cash on this darned car lately.

It had been her mother's years ago. It was about all she had left of her mother. Pip had her mother's diamond earrings. Phoebe had her engagement ring to pass down one day. Pan had the necklace her father had given her mother on their twentieth wedding anniversary. Perci had a small bracelet that had been her mother's graduation present from her parents. Her mother had given it to her when she'd graduated her nursing program, shortly before her mother had died.

That bracelet and her mother's car were hers. She was going to drive that car until it fell apart around her.

She stepped on something next to her tire. A coffee cup. She grabbed it, walked it to the trash can nearby, then hurried back to her car—out of the rain.

When the engine refused to turn over, she cursed. Perci knew what had most likely happened. The seal on her tank wasn't great. Rain had probably leaked right into her gas tank. She had no idea what to do with water in the tank.

It was no doubt going to be right back to the

mechanic's. She tried again, then again one more time.

Finally, it started.

With her fingers crossed that it would hold out until she got to the ranch, she pulled out of the parking lot.

Fifteen minutes later and she knew it was more than just a little water in her tank. Something was seriously going on.

Every time she accelerated, the car jolted.

When she rounded the curve where her mother had died and the car sputtered, it was all Perci could do to keep it on the road.

Her front end went off into the shallowest part of the ditch—ten feet from the worst part of the road.

Ten feet from where her mother had been hurt.

The crosses on the hill above her cast rain-drenched shadows on the pavement below.

Perci carefully avoided standing in those shadows while she dialed the only number she could remember.

Her fingers hit speed dial for *him* instinctively. Nate.

She wanted Nate. She knew he would come for her without question.

After she disconnected, she was finally able to ask herself *why*.

Unfortunately, she didn't have an answer.

20

THE IDEA THAT SHE COULD HAVE BEEN HURT had him feeling more than a little raw. As did the knowledge that she had only called him because she had been on her way to pick up Ivy. He wanted her to call him for *anything* she needed.

When he pulled up behind her car, she was standing out next to it. Her red hair hung down her back in a soggy mess. Tyler blue eyes met his. Nate fought the urge to scoop her up and just hold her close for a minute or five hundred. "I'm beginning to think this car is cursed."

"It's past its prime. I don't doubt it." He didn't say anything more. Perci couldn't afford a new car, and he knew it. He knew exactly how much she made on the hour—and he knew where most of it went. Groceries. Bills.

To support her family. Even now that her sisters had married his brothers, they all still pitched in to support their family. He'd made certain, along with Levi, that her car was in the best shape he could make it when his youngest brother had offered to give it a tune-up for her. She didn't know that Nate had helped, but he had. He'd even purchased half the parts for it himself. For her. "What happened?"

"I'm not certain. A belt, I think. But it's the one that runs beneath everything, and I can't see out here."

"We'll hitch it to my truck, and I'll tow it back to your father's ranch. I can get Matt out, and we'll both take a look at it this weekend. In the meantime, Pan's is still sitting in the drive." His brother had bought her sister a small SUV. With Pan in Hollywood at the moment, it was just sitting there.

And it was a hell of a lot safer than Perci's little car.

He made quick work of hitching the car to the back of his truck. It would have to be flat-towed. Not the best option in the rain, but they were only twenty miles down a mostly deserted road. Her father's place was at the end of that twenty miles, and she had a few uncles and cousins in between. They shouldn't pass too many other cars—and those they did would most likely all be Tylers.

Some of his tension lessened. He might not have liked many of her male cousins because of previous interactions, but he'd say this for them—they took care of each other. She'd have been ok.

It was just hard for him not to worry about her. To want to protect.

They climbed into the cab of his truck. He grabbed a blanket from the backseat and tossed it at her. "Cover up. I'll turn the heater on. You look half drowned."

"I feel half drowned. The car slid. It got a little hairy there."

His tension flooded back. Nate tightened his hands on the wheel. "You sure you're ok?"

She nodded. "I just don't like driving at night in the rain."

Because of her mother, no doubt. He hadn't missed the cross standing above her car on that hill. "You're ok, now, baby. I promise."

He'd never meant anything more than what he said right then.

She visibly shivered again. Nate shocked the

both of them when he pulled her against his chest and held her for a moment.

Thin arms went around him, and she pressed even closer.

"I know. Thank you for coming to get me."

"Anytime you need me, I'll be right here." Nate looked down into Tyler blue eyes. "I mean that."

His world shifted just a little to the left when he realized that having her in his arms was the most *right* thing he'd ever felt.

Perci had fast become his world, and Nate had just accepted it two hundred percent.

21

SHE WAS FINALLY STARTING TO RELAX. THE instant he'd pulled up—and she'd known he would, from the moment she'd decided to call him, and not his brothers—some of the fear and tension had left her. He'd looked so big and strong and perfect when he'd climbed out. Ready to conquer the world.

Or at least help her out.

She *should* have called her father. Or anyone other than him. They would have been closer. Easier. But it had been Nate who she'd wanted to call the most.

So she'd called him. And there he was. No questions asked. He'd just...come for her.

Just like she'd known he would. "I called my dad after I spoke with you. He's home now."

He pulled in to her father's drive and backed her car into the space in front of what remained of the small barn. It had once been the oldest structure on their property, built by her great-grandfather.

Until Jay Gunderson had burned it down.

Every time she looked at it, she was reminded of what had happened. The investigation was finally over. They were just waiting on the insurance money to have it removed.

She couldn't wait.

Perci still had nightmares about that barn. The moment when she'd known her twin sister was going to die had been one of the worst moments of her life—it had her waking in a cold sweat more nights than not. And nauseated.

No doubt Pip was having similar dreams, too. They always did.

Or they used to, when they shared every single day together.

She missed her twin more than she had ever thought possible, but she was thrilled Pip was so happy. Matt beyond adored her sister. And that was what mattered.

They were all happy.

It was only Perci that still felt *off*.

Maybe it was only she that was having the nightmares.

"Stay there. I'll get you over the mud."

"I'm ok."

"You're wearing your tennis shoes. Stay."

She stayed, even though she didn't like him being so heavy-handed. He opened her door, and before she knew it, hot hands were wrapped around her waist.

Nate guided her out of his ridiculously big farm truck like she was helpless and swung her over the mud. Her father really needed to get the driveway regraveled whenever they got the money.

Thunder cracked overhead, and lightning shot across the sky. Perci squeaked like an idiot.

Nate's hands tightened on her waist, and just like that, he pulled her flush up against his chest. "You all right?"

Oh, yeah. Being held by a gorgeous, strong, kindhearted man who'd rushed through the storm to rescue her was never going to be all wrong. Perci wasn't stupid.

She most definitely *was* attracted to this man.

He had the power to change everything about

her world, and she damned well knew it. "I'm ok. Just ready to get home."

He snorted. "You *are* home."

She'd meant...heck, she didn't know what she meant. "Don't be a butt. I meant..."

Nate's hands tightened on her waist and lifted. Until they were almost mouth to mouth, with the rain pouring down all around them. He kissed her and pulled back so quickly she almost thought she'd imagined it. Then he swung her down to the grass next to the drive. "Let's get inside before we blow away."

He wrapped a hot hand around hers and pulled her to the door of the only home she had ever known.

Her fingers fumbled on the door. Nate shifted to block the pouring rain from her.

Protecting.

Why did he always feel the need to protect her? So many times in the last year or so he had done whatever he could to put himself between her and any danger that existed out there.

She'd noticed it each and every time. And each and every time she didn't know how to feel. It seemed like they'd fought so much.

Or...they used to. They hadn't in recent weeks.

She was just so tired of fighting everything anymore.

It felt like she'd been fighting since the night her entire world had changed alongside a dangerous, rain-slicked mountain road.

Sometimes the only thing that had kept her going was *fighting*.

She pushed open the door and stepped into the entrance of her home. She, Pan, and Pip had rearranged the furniture a bit after both Phoebe and Phoenix had moved out. Nothing had changed since Pan and Pip had left themselves, though. Perci hadn't wanted it to.

Her oldest sister was sprawled in the floor, their youngest brother Parker next to her. Ivy was spread out on the floor, giggling.

Perci smiled instinctively at the happy sound. Ivy didn't laugh often, but when she did, it was contagious. "Hey, is this a private party?"

Ivy squealed and rolled to her belly. She jumped up in that springy way kids had and hurled herself toward Perci. "*Mama Perci! Mama!*"

Before Perci could blink, she had an armful of little girl. Perci hugged her back, trying to keep up with the excited babble. She'd process the *mama* later. "Hi, baby. Did you have fun with Phoebe?"

"Aunt Pee-be can't hear Ivy good. I have to *yell*. And Pee-be no *hit* for yelling."

"Nobody hits for yelling here. Nobody gets to hit here ever. I promise." She hugged Ivy then gasped when the little girl dove toward the man next to her.

"*Daddy* Nate!"

Nate's hands were there to catch the little girl, as if Ivy had known they would be. Tears sprang to Perci's eyes at the way the trust in the child's actions was just so...there. Ivy was trusting them.

Just like Perci was beginning to trust *him*.

Her whole world rocked on its axis when her eyes rose to his.

22

JUDITH HOPEWELL PULLED INTO THE Masterson ranch and took a long look around. This was her first visit to this part of the county, though she had certainly heard of the four Masterson brothers. Every woman knew about the Masterson brothers. Gossip just saw to that far too easily.

She knew the sheriff from her work as one of the only three social workers assigned to the entire Masterson County area, though she normally handled cases in the northern part of the county.

He was a nice man, good at his job, and fair in his dealings with everyone.

This was the second time she'd met his brother, the doctor. He had a file with her office, but only in a good way. He and his three brothers had all been approved as foster parents for teenage boys in need. She just hoped what she was about to find worked out well for all of them.

They didn't have a single available bed for an almost three-year-old girl anywhere within the county. Everyone in the town was either unable to take on another child, or they weren't approved for an additional child or one that age. All she could hope for was that the Masterson family was willing, at least for the time being.

Levi Masterson was the foster parent on record, but his brothers had been approved, as well. Their wives hadn't yet, but that could be remedied quickly, if needed. It was the best situation she could hope for. On paper, anyway.

What was happening inside that house remained to be seen. If Ivy wasn't adjusting or wasn't safe, then she would have to be moved. It wasn't Jude's first choice, but she'd made it before. Some foster homes were better equipped for different ages than others.

Sometimes all she did lately was make the difficult choices.

She wasn't certain how much longer she was going to be able to do this job. Far too many times lately, it had been the kids who were the ones who ultimately lost.

A truck pulled in behind her. Jude turned toward it.

A big man handsome enough to make even her immune heart pound for a second stepped out of the driver's side. A small redhead exited from the passenger side. The woman immediately went toward the backseat.

A blond-haired child clung to her when the woman stepped back.

Ivy.

Jude took a moment to study the little girl that she had known about for well over a year now. Had been waiting to help for most of that time.

It wasn't the first time she'd met Ivy North. Nor did she suspect it would be the last time. Now, though, she hoped it would be a better future for the little one than she'd predicted before. Ivy's parents hadn't stepped over the line enough for immediate intervention. They'd had to go through other processes first.

Until *this* time.

Ivy was babbling to the woman carrying her— Jude vaguely recognized her as a nurse from the hospital that she'd seen a time or two, but never spoken to—and Jude could hear the giggles over the sound of the rain.

She'd never heard Ivy giggle like that.

The little girl had been with the Mastersons for three days now. Apparently, it was helping.

Some of the tension and worry Jude had felt about having the girl placed in a home she herself hadn't vetted lessened.

She stepped off the porch toward the big man and held out her hand. "Dr. Masterson? I'm here for Ivy."

23

NATE'S HEART FROZE FOR A MOMENT. HE watched Perci's arms tighten around the little girl who it was obvious she adored, like she was never going to let Ivy go. He put his hand on her back to reassure, though if the social worker was truly there to take the girl, there wasn't anything he or Perci could do.

"In what way?" he asked, as Perci hurried up the steps and carried Ivy inside out of the rain. The social worker, a dark-haired woman a few years older than Perci and a few inches taller, smiled. She had a pretty smile, and big green eyes behind thick-rimmed glasses. Pretty, but terrifying.

She held Ivy's future in her hands, and he knew it.

"I'm here to check that Ivy is settling in all right, and get some paperwork taken care of."

He ushered the woman inside behind Perci. Perci had already sat Ivy on the couch and was pulling her little raincoat off. "I think she's doing well. She's healing. During the day when Perci and I are working, she's staying with Perci's sister, my sister-in-law Phoebe. The sheriff's wife."

"Is Perci living here, then?" The social worker glanced toward the two in the living room.

He knew what she saw.

"No. She's staying to help Ivy adjust, at least until her sister Pan arrives. Perci was the nurse most often in contact with Ivy, and the two had bonded. Since she's family, and has stayed here before, it has worked out well." He didn't know what to say. He wanted what was best for the little girl more than anything. "Is there another family available? Anyone from her birth family?"

The social worker hesitated. "Mrs. North is going to prison for a long time, Dr. Masterson. Not only for charges in this state, and Montana, but she skipped bail in Colorado on aggravated assault charges four years ago. She'll be extradited there.

We've already spoken with her, and she's decided to sign a termination of parental rights form. We'll be identifying an adoptive family for Ivy as soon as that's finished."

"No biological relatives?"

"None identified as suitable candidates. That can change as we go through the process, of course, but Mrs. North indicated that she is an only child with no close relatives and her husband was a ward of the state of Texas. So...barring any sudden barriers, she'll go up for adoption as soon as we can make it happen. It should be an easy transition, as she's healthy and...young."

He understood; the sooner Ivy was adopted, the sooner she would have stability.

The little girl came barreling into the kitchen. "Mama Perci has to potty."

Nate scooped her up, inhaling the scent of clean child and cookies. Phoebe had no doubt given her cookies at some point today.

Ivy snuggled against his chest and eyed the social worker warily. "Who you?"

Nate rubbed her back gently. He knew she was afraid. He could feel it. "This is Ms. Hopewell, little Miss Ivy. She's here to check on you."

Ivy just blinked. "Want Mama Perci to hold me."

PERCI RETURNED TO THE KITCHEN IN TIME TO hear Ivy's demand. Her first instinct was to take Ivy from Nate and just hold her tight. So she did. She wasn't ready for the idea that this woman in the middle of Nate's kitchen could take Ivy and spirit her away.

Ivy's stay with the Mastersons was temporary.

Even though Ivy just seemed to fit.

Belonged. Ivy almost seemed to belong right where she was.

Perci settled Ivy into the booster seat her father had found in the attic of their home and grabbed a washcloth. Ivy's hands needed washed, before anything else.

Dinner was simple enough to prep, thanks to Pan's obsessive need to plan everything. It was right there in the fridge, waiting

She busied herself the best she could. "How long?"

The woman looked at her. "Excuse me?"

"How long will it take before she has a more

permanent home? She's settling in here. She's comfortable. Safe. I'd hate to see that disrupted, if she's just going to sit in foster care for a while." It was a crazy idea, but her first instinct was to take the little girl herself. Do what she had to in order to get Ivy at her father's ranch.

The idea was as crazy as any other she'd ever had.

Her home wouldn't compare to one with a mom and dad. An established family that didn't struggle to buy peanut butter, let alone new tires for her eighteen-year-old car.

Ivy deserved more than what Perci could give her—even if they would let her have her.

Ivy would be better off staying right where she was. But that would put a huge burden on Pan, who was just now settling in with her new husband.

Another family would be the best fit, no matter how much it hurt to think about. For Ivy, Pan, and Levi.

In just the span of three days Perci had fallen in love with that little girl, and she wouldn't deny it.

"We'll try our very best to make sure she's with people who love her."

24

JUDE COULD READ THE PRETTY REDHEAD LIKE
an open book. Perci Tyler was one of those who
did love that little girl.

The other was the man looking at Perci like
she was his entire world. Did Perci realize that?

Jude knew the story of the Masterson brothers
and the women who they had married. She knew
the rumors about these two, too.

If all went as everyone assumed it was going,
they'd be married soon, too.

What could it hurt for Ivy to find her home
with them? They were already bonding. It was in
the way the child looked at them. The way they
looked at her.

The way they looked at each other.

Jude had seen many families in her four years as a social worker. Mostly at the worst times in their lives. She'd seen kids in such appalling conditions *she* still had nightmares where those kids weren't rescued in time.

Ivy had been one of those kids, but her mother had never *quite* crossed over the line until now. And background checks under the woman's name hadn't turned up anything initially. Until the sheriff had given her the woman's aliases, as well as arrest reports going back more than a decade.

Jude would be questioning the other women in her office on how that had been missed, the first chance she got.

Now it had all come to a head.

Leaving Ivy blowing in the wind.

Jude took a quick, surreptitious look around.

This home was a good one. Comfortable and welcoming. Perfect for a child to grow up in.

If she had the right parents, of course.

"Dr. Masterson, you're a state-approved foster parent, I believe?" She knew he was. She'd made it a point to know everything she could about the man before she'd stepped foot on his property today.

"Yes. For teenagers. Boys."

"We can amend that now. If you are prepared to assume full responsibility for Ivy until an adoptive placement can be found?" It could take up to two years before that happened. Jude knew the statistics far too well. She hated the idea that the little girl could potentially be bounced around for that long. They were taking some liberties today, but she would handle it. It was in the best interests of the child, after all. Which was all she was really after. "It can take several months for that to happen. Would you be able to manage?"

"Between our two families, he'll manage." Perci had Ivy in her arms again. The little girl was obviously enjoying having the cuddles. "If he...wanted."

The look Perci shot the doctor broadcast everything the woman was feeling.

Jude felt for her—she truly did.

And Nate Masterson was apparently putty in Perci Tyler's hands. "Ivy will be welcome here as long as needed."

If Jude hadn't sworn off romance of any kind, she'd be envious of the other woman. To have a man like that look at you in that way...well, Perci was one lucky woman. No doubt about that.

25

RHEA PLACED THE LETTER SHAMELESSLY IN front of her son, enjoying the perturbed look he'd sent her. She'd shown up a few minutes after she'd known he'd be out of bed, on the excuse that the letter had come to her house instead of his by mistake.

She'd snagged it out of the mail yesterday. She'd gotten enough of those damned service-to-the-community-awards envelopes from Masterson to know exactly what it most likely was. Someone on the hospital staff got one every year, it seemed.

It was perfect.

Nate would have to go, of course, and he would need an escort.

He opened it and read it with the irritation she'd expected from her surliest son. She hadn't resorted to opening the letter, of course. But she knew...

Perci was at the stove, making breakfast for Ivy. Rhea took a moment to study the girl. She was such a pretty little thing, with just enough fire to combat Nate's fierceness. The two were good for each other. Why wouldn't they just admit that?

"You'll need an escort, of course. I suppose you can ask one of your sisters-in-law, but that might be a bit too confusing. And I'm sure Phoebe and Joel are already going. Pan may not even be in town. Perci, would your twin be willing to spend the evening with Nate at the country club?"

"Probably not."

"So, unless Nate has someone in mind, I can go. Unless...Perci, would you be willing to go with Nate and represent the hospital?" Rhea sent a smile at the girl. "It would save him from the embarrassment of going with his mother."

"I can get my own dates just fine, Mother." Nate's irritation was clear. "Perci may be busy that night."

"Not with that attitude you won't. What woman

would have you?" Rhea sent a bland smile at him next, then reached over to brush the blond curls of her future grandbaby. Ivy gave a shy smile in return.

"When is it?" Perci asked, her wariness very evident. Her son saw her as irritating at the moment, meddling. But Perci...her future daughter-in-law knew exactly what Rhea's intentions were. Suspicious girl, this one. More so than the others.

Now, how was she supposed to use that against the two of them? "I would happily stay here with the little one. You two go represent the hospital we all love. As the next generation. Your father and I went so many times." Rhea let herself get choked up, knowing it would push her son's buttons perfectly. Nate was such a sensitive, compassionate soul under all that gruff. "I don't know that I can go again. Not so soon."

Daniel was probably spinning in his grave, seeing what she was doing to their boy, but it was worth it. Her husband would want her sons to be *happy*. The same way *they* had been.

Nate wasn't truly happy. Not yet. He was just too alone. But Rhea had a plan.

She shot another look at the young woman across the room. Yes. She'd guessed right. The compassion in Perci Tyler was enough to have the girl falling in line exactly as Rhea needed.

She masked her satisfaction by bending over and kissing Ivy's sweet little blond curls. A sweet new daughter-in-law, a precious new grandchild—what more could a woman ask for?

26

THE LAST TIME SHE HAD HAD A DATE WAS TWO
months before her mother had died. It had been
with Thomas Jacobi, a nice boy a few years older
than her then twenty. He'd married a girl two
counties over six months later. They already had
four kids, and she'd heard there was another on
the way.

Thomas had never made her feel like this.

And it wasn't even a *real* date.

To be honest, she didn't know what she was
doing. Or why she had gone to the trouble of bor-
rowing a dress from Phoebe.

Phoebe, who had attended several events with

her husband, had had far more appropriate clothing than Perci now.

She didn't want to embarrass Nate, or the hospital, by arriving in any of her well-worn dress clothes. She usually only wore them to church. And they were starting to show their age and abuse from the multiple washings they'd endured.

But the blue dress she'd borrowed from her sister—that was cut way lower than anything Perci had ever worn before—was perfect for an evening at the Masterson Country Club.

Country clubs weren't exactly where *Tylers* belonged. Unless they were on staff. She thought her cousin Maggie had worked at the country club for about a month a few years ago—before Maggie's brothers had shown up and gotten her fired.

Perci had never been at the country club before. The mere idea of it had her feeling a bit more nervous than she wanted to admit.

Even if her sister had done just fine the times she'd been there with Joel.

She finished her hair and makeup and stepped out of the room she'd been using.

Nate waited in the kitchen with his mother and Ivy.

Perci stepped closer and brushed a kiss against

Ivy's blond hair. The little girl had jelly on her fingers. Nate scooped Ivy up before that jelly could get on Perci's dress. "Hang on, kiddo. Let's clean you up. We don't want to mess up that pretty dress."

"*Bootibul.*"

"Yes, she is." Nate shot a look at her out of those Masterson green eyes of his. A look filled with more heat than Perci wanted to think about. "Very nice."

"Not so bad yourself." Talk about understatement. Nate filled out his tux in ways made to cause a woman to lose her breath. She'd seen him in a tux before.

Each time he'd looked better than the last.

"You are going to be the most stunning couple there."

Perci had forgotten his mother was there while she was staring at Nate. Heat hit her cheeks. She'd just ogled the man, in front of his mother. Pitiful. "Thank you."

His mother smiled. "You two had better go. The guest of honor can't be late."

Perci just felt like an idiot when she nodded. There really wasn't anything else to say.

NATE'S EVENING WAS TEDIOUS, AND HE KNEW it. The only bright spot at all was the woman at his side. Perci had been greeted by many that he knew she didn't know, but she'd held her own. Charmed the lot of them.

Probably a bit too much. Nate scowled when an obviously tipsy relative of the mayor tried to look down that blue dress.

He recognized it, of course. Her sister had worn it before. But never had he drooled over Phoebe because of it.

On the slightly taller Perci, it was just a bit shorter and a bit more daringly cut. Perfect.

He wanted to ditch this event and take her somewhere where he could explain to her what that dress did to a man like him.

What would she do if he did just that?

He was still watching her when she excused herself and headed to the restroom. She sent him a look and a smile, and held up her hand, indicating she would be with him again in five minutes.

He smiled back.

It was so much nicer when they weren't fighting each other.

He watched her cross the room, her red hair easy to spot in the crowd.

27

Clive sat at his table and watched the crowd. He'd been a member of this country club since before Perci Tyler had even been born. His membership had almost been revoked a time or two, but he was still a member. Barely.

Since the Mastersons had taken everything from him.

But there *she* was. A damned Tyler. Right in the middle of everyone who mattered in this county.

Her sister was there somewhere, clinging to the new sheriff like a damned limpet. The two had charmed every bigwig in the county, with that

girl's different way of talking and those big blue
eyes of hers.

No doubt securing funding for the sheriff's next
run for office in a few years or for the hospital itself.

Nate Masterson, the doctor who had let Jay
suffer and *die*, had been honored for all of his good
work for the county. The whole evening had been
about Mastersons, practically.

Shit.

Damned Mastersons were taking *everything*.

While *he* was stuck at a table with Clint and
Maria.

The boy was also being honored for his recent
bravery during an arrest Clint had made. Clive
was proud; of course, he was. Or so he told himself. Clint was a damned fine nephew and not a
half-bad stepson, even if Clint had definite opin-
ions that didn't always match Clive's.

Clint would never be Jay.

And they both knew it.

That doctor had overshadowed what *his*
stepson had accomplished.

Mastersons were taking *everything*.

It would serve that doctor right if someone
took everything *he* had away, too.

28

Nate watched her walk across the room, thinking how much he wanted that woman. And not just because of outward appearance. It was the way she breathed fire at him, the way she made him feel, the way she terrified him right out of his tux.

He would always burn for Perci, and he didn't think that was going to change anytime soon.

Someone bumped him while he was staring at her.

Nate turned. Clint Gunderson was standing too damned close.

Nate tensed immediately. He never personally had had anything against Clive Gunderson's oldest son. The guy seemed like a decent sort. Joel hadn't mentioned any problems with the man, either.

As far as Nate knew, Clint stuck to himself, working for the Wyoming Highway Patrol and part-time ranching somewhere in the northeastern part of the county.

"Gunderson, didn't see you standing there."

"No problem. Noticed you came with one of the Tyler girls. She doing okay? Healed all right?"

Nate's attention sharpened. "She's fine. They all are. *We're* seeing to that."

The other man held up a hand. They'd gone to school together, him and Clint. They hadn't been friends, but they had known each other. "I meant nothing by it. Just concern. I know those girls didn't have a damn thing to do with what my idiot brother did. And I'm sorry that I didn't see it. Not in time to help, anyway. I knew my brother had some problems, but I'd never imagined he would go off the deep end like that. Or be so obsessed with your sister-in-law. I want your family and the Tylers to know that I am genuinely sorry for what he did. Hell, for what I learned my father did to them, too. I wasn't even living in the county when Jay attacked that girl back then the first time. I

didn't know about any of it. I know it's not an excuse, but I want you to know that I have no ill will
toward those girls at all."

There was genuine regret in Gunderson's eyes.
Gunderson looked past Nate's shoulder and
cursed. Nate turned to follow his gaze. That's
when he saw two beautiful redheads, practically
cornered near the back of the room by none other
than Clint's father.

Both men started across the room. It took all
Nate had not to make a scene. He looked for his
brother, surprised that Joel wasn't right there at
Phoebe's side already. Joel took overprotective to
the next level.

He found his brother stuck between several
local councilmen. Joel was not going anywhere for
a while. His brother caught his eye and jerked his
head toward Phoebe and Perci. Nate nodded.

He'd get his sister-in-law away from Gunderson as fast as possible. And Perci.

The look Perci sent him when he approached
told its own story. He held out a hand to her, while
dropping the other on Phoebe's narrow shoulder.
Gunderson was not going to do anything to hurt
the women he cared about ever again. "Sweetheart? *Gunderson*."

PERCI STEPPED IN FRONT OF PHOEBE WITHOUT thought. But it wasn't her older sister that Gunderson had fixated on. It was her. Clive Gunderson looked at her just like he had the night her mother had died, and in the dozens of times he'd pulled her over since.

She would *never* share the terror that had filled her those late nights when he'd harassed her. Shortly before he'd lost the election to Joel, he'd made her get out of her car and kneel in the mud while he'd searched her car.

Searched *her*.

After that incident, it had gotten to the point where she'd almost asked her father to pick her up each night.

But if she had, she'd have had to explain *why*.

Her father wouldn't have stopped until he'd killed Gunderson for what he was doing to her. Perci had known that without a shadow of a doubt.

Gunderson's eyes burned with the hatred she had seen before. She was just about to say something to him, when a large male body moved closer. She knew who it was without having to look first.

Nate was there. Just like she had known he would be.

The instant Gunderson had cornered her and Phoebe, Perci had looked for him. And found him. He had already been on his way to her side. The knowledge that he was coming to her had helped strengthen her spine and made it easier for her to look at the man who had flat out told her that her mother had deserved to die. Nate was there. She wasn't dealing with this alone, even though her sister was right next to her.

She trusted him.

Would always trust him. Even though he irritated her more than any man on earth ever had. She trusted him, and she always would.

That thought hit her like a bullet.

A little thrill of something went straight through her. He held out a hand to her, and she took it without hesitation. *Now* she could deal with Clive Gunderson. Without the fear that she had hidden from her family for so long.

They all had their nightmares. Clive Gunderson had been in hers for the last four years.

29

CLIVE FORCED HIMSELF TO BREATHE, TO behave himself. Clint was watching him like a hawk. His stepson wasn't stupid; that was one thing the boy had going for him.

Clint was probably the smartest Gunderson in a long time.

Clive wanted to tell that girl exactly what he thought of her. To rip into her, put her back in her place, exactly where she deserved to be. Tylers were trash; had always been. He'd arrested more Tylers in his county during his tenure as sheriff than any other family. Good arrests, deserved arrests; Tylers were trouble. Every last one of them.

These girls were no different.

Why didn't the rest of the town see that?

Clint drove him home. Boy didn't say much until they were almost there. "You need to leave those Tylers alone. Those girls are not responsible for what Jay did. He made the choices. I've read the reports. I've been to the scene myself. *Jay* did it. Not those women. You need to be apologizing to them instead of harassing them. It was damn lucky that Perci and her twin and Masterson's brother weren't killed in the fire. Did you know a beam fell on the twins? A burning beam from a fire *Jay* set. Hell, if you were still sheriff, you'd have had to arrest him. Did you know that Pip and Matt went back in to get Jay? They could've left him to burn. And they didn't. Those girls will always have the scars from what he did. They don't need you making things worse. Leave her and her sisters alone. I mean it. You harass them in any way. and I'll arrest you myself on something. Mark my words; I'm not joking with this. Enough."

Clive didn't say anything. No matter what Clint said, those girls *were* responsible for Jay. If Jay hadn't seen them four years ago, his son would still be alive. That was indisputable.

"Those Tylers are trouble. Don't you go looking in that direction. They may look nice, but they get men killed." Tom Rutherford and Jay were indisputable proof of that.

Clint snorted. "I have no intention of looking at a Tyler woman. No matter how she gets under my skin. I don't intend to look at a woman again for a very long time. I got problems of my own that I need to deal with first. But even if that wasn't the case, a man would be damned lucky to get one of those girls. They are hard workers, kind, and loyal. Not to mention the whole lot of them are beautiful. They don't need you making trouble for them. Not like you did before."

Clive looked at the boy. Thinking once again how much like Clive's younger brother he looked.

How can anyone not look at the boy and realize that this man was not Clive's son but his nephew? Of course, he had covered the truth of Clint's parentage up since the boy had been born. He didn't see that changing anytime soon. He didn't have his son anymore, but he had his nephew—who also happened to be his stepson. Why couldn't he be happy with that? At least content.

Clint was all the blood relation Clive had left in the world—him and that baby girl.

Clive would never get Jay back. It was time he accepted that.

Because Clint would never be Jay. There were no other words to be said. Clint was never going to be his son. Because those damn Tyler women and those Mastersons had taken Jay away from him forever.

He didn't have anything else to say until Clint dropped him off in front of his house. Clive had no intention of going in. He needed to get out. Underneath the Wyoming sky. To breathe. To think. He needed to do something.

Something to get the rage inside of him out. He just drove. Until he ended up right outside the country club. He waited until he saw the doctor's truck go by, Masterson and that redheaded bitch inside.

Clive followed them.

And wept.

30

SHE WAS QUIETER THAN HE WAS USED TO. Nate threw a glance at her. "You okay? He didn't upset you too badly, did he?"

She looked at him. He couldn't see her in the darkness of the cab, but he suspected she smirked at him in that particular *Perci* way she had. "There's nothing Clive Gunderson could throw out that I can't handle."

"I don't have any doubt about that." Still, she was like a hissing kitten facing a rattlesnake. Gunderson was far more dangerous than that. The idea that the sonofabitch had even *looked* at Perci sideways tonight pissed him off. "But I don't trust him, and I don't like how he was looking at you."

"I'm not going to talk about *him*. Isn't that the ranch you are moving into soon?" She pointed to the gate just a bit up the road from them.

"Yes. It's almost ready." When it was, he had no more excuses not to move in. Not that he had any question that he wanted to move to the home that was his. But with Perci and Ivy at Levi's, Nate wasn't in any true hurry. Not now.

Not unless he could bring her with him. *Them,* with him.

Impulse had him turning toward that gate. It had an electronic lock on it, and he had the remote in his glovebox. With a few movements he had the gate swinging right open.

"What are we doing?" she asked as he pulled the truck up in front of the three-story farmhouse that had been in his family for over one hundred years now.

He'd had new siding installed just last week.

"Just going to check the place. And you and I are going to talk without my mother overhearing. Or meddling. You don't mind, do you?" He was in no hurry to take her back to Levi's. He was especially in no hurry to be on the end of his mother's knowing glances. Or to give Perci back over to the little girl who adored her.

No. He wanted the woman with him for himself for a while. Nate didn't see a damn thing wrong with that.

Did she mind? Not at all. Perci had made her decision when Clive Gunderson had so clearly illustrated the difference between a man like him and one like Nate.

When she had realized that she did trust Nate to be there when she needed him. That no matter what she said or did, he was there. All she had to do was take the hand he had held out.

She *wanted* him to be the man she depended on. The one she turned to when the world they faced got a little too grim for her to handle it alone. Not that she *needed* him. She could certainly survive without him.

But he gave her world a bit more fire than it had had for a long time.

It was time she went after what she wanted. A hot curl of anticipation went right through her.

Nate Masterson had no idea what was about to hit him.

She followed him up the driveway and onto

the front porch. She hadn't seen this property before, but keeping up with the places the Masterson brothers owned was nearly impossible. Levi owned several places, Matt was half owner in a few others with Levi, Matt owned his own horse ranch nearby, and Joel had a larger home nearer to town than the others and was also a part owner in all the others. She had never asked what *Nate* was involved in.

"Nice place." It was four times the size of the house she lived in. There was a barn behind the house that was also in the process of being painted. She'd heard he'd been redoing the entire house to his exact specifications.

It was beautiful. It was also huge for a single man. Empty.

"It was my great-grandparents'. We bought it back a year ago. Levi manages the land around the house, but the house is mine." There was real satisfaction in his words that she understood.

"You're lucky. Our parents bought our ranch when Phoebe was a baby. On contract. They paid it off when I was eighteen. We've been making improvements bit by bit." And it was getting there. Things were finally less tight, thanks to the initial

settlement check the insurance company had issued the month before.

It wasn't enough. And her father was talking
about hiring an attorney with that money to ensure
everything was handled the way it was supposed
to be. Rectified. As much as it could be, anyway.

They'd finally had enough money to paint the
exterior of the ranch, thanks to that check, and the
money they'd earned being in Rowland Bowles's
movie.

Perci winced even thinking about what she'd
had to do as a damned fairy princess in search of
her lost twin.

But other than the premiere, she had no more
obligations in that direction.

For the first time in a long while, she could
breathe again. She *didn't* have to work sixty hours
a week for her family to barely squeak by. She
didn't have to worry any longer.

Some of the fear that had plagued her since
the night her mother had died shifted. Lessened.

"I have some soda in the fridge. Not the
healthiest of drinks, but I won't tell if you won't."

She nodded. He didn't have the place furnished
except for a couch shoved up in front of the large

front window. She could see the moon and stars—and the hills that separated them from the rest of his and Levi's property. To imagine that the Masterson brothers owned everything in between was slightly overwhelming. Her family's ranch was but a very tiny ranch in the scheme of things in Wyoming.

But it was home. The only home Perci had ever known.

"Thank you."

He went into the kitchen, then returned. She watched him move, sudden nerves keeping her from acting on what she'd wanted in the truck.

It was one thing to be ready to be with a man; it was another for her to know how to make that desire known.

She masked her nerves by sinking onto the surprisingly comfortable couch. He followed her down. "We won't stay long. I'm just not ready to deal with my mother tonight."

She laughed lightly. "Afraid?"

"Of her? Definitely. No doubt she's put Ivy to bed and is snooping through the house. I can't wait until Pan's back and gets custody of Mother. It's bound to be hilarious."

"Should I call my sister and warn her? Tell her that even the big bad Nate is afraid of his mother?"

"Don't you dare. We figure Pan is the only one brave enough to deal with her—your sister married Levi, after all."

"Funny."

Sitting on a couch in formal wear with Nate Masterson beside her. Not a single bit of it made sense. "What are we really doing here?"

"We're going to talk. You're going to tell me why the very sight of Clive Gunderson makes you pale and shake and lose every bit of fire I know you have in you. What did he do to *you* that your family doesn't know about?"

31

PERCI IMMEDIATELY STARTED SHIVERING, though Nate's house wasn't all that cold. She jumped up and moved to the window to stare out at the dark rain. "I don't want to talk about it."

Nate's hands landed on her shoulders, and he turned her.

A warm, big hand cupped her cheek. He brushed her lip lightly with his thumb. "He hurt you?"

Hurt her? No. Just terrified her each and every time she got behind the wheel of her car. Just shattered every hope she'd had of peace and safety. "He never actually touched me. Except once. One night when I refused to get out of my car, he yanked me out. Held me against the hood. But it's over now."

"Is it? I don't like how he was looking at you tonight."

"He's just a bully who gets off on scaring people. After...after Jay attacked Pip at the community center, Gunderson showed up to threaten us. Phoebe...she tried to stand up to him, Nate. So did I. Pan...Pan was just a kid and was fighting mad, but Gunderson left her alone for the most part. He...I think he confused me and Pip that first day he came out. So I let him."

"Protecting your twin. Like you always do." He dropped his hands to encircle her waist. Before she knew it, Perci was leaning against him in front of the large glass window. "Tell me. Help me understand."

"I smarted off something to him about his son being a pervert with a bad attitude, or something. I thought he was going to hit me, but my uncle drove up to deliver some goats to Phoebe." He didn't say anything, just letting her talk. Words poured out in a way they hadn't in a long while. "He was just *everywhere* after that. I don't know if he thought I was Pip, and by scaring her, she'd keep quiet, or if it was something I'd done, but he was always there.

I had some night classes across the county line. He started following me home every Thursday. Then it was Tuesdays, too."

"Did you tell anyone? Report him?"

"Tell who? Report him to whom? There weren't a whole lot of options for me, Nate. I know that. Until Joel took over as sheriff, he followed me home from work *every* single week. Then I didn't know when he would be out there. But he would be. Just waiting. He went in to the sheriff's office at six a.m. But at three thirty, he was out there, waiting for *me*."

NATE BIT BACK THE RAGE—AND THE GUILT. She'd worked for *him* for four months before Joel had been elected. On the night shift. He hadn't known. If he had, he'd have damned well driven home with her one night and dealt with Clive Gunderson himself. Showed the bastard what it was like to be vulnerable like that. How Joel had managed to deal with Gunderson when they'd worked together, Nate would never understand. But his brother had. For at least a year before winning the position.

During that time, Gunderson was using his position to terrify Perci.

"He's been stalking and harassing you for four years?"

"Not since Joel. He stopped then. And he stopped for about three months when my mother died. But every time I'd see him in town, he'd gloat that he got us. That *he* held all the power."

"He's a bastard, honey." Nate would be talking to Joel first chance he got. See if there was something that could be done now. To make sure she was safe. "He's never going to get close enough to you to hurt you ever again."

Nate pulled her toward the couch and then down onto his lap. He wasn't ready to let go of her yet. He suspected she felt the same way.

"Is he? He hates us, especially now."

"I'm not going to let him. From now on, you'll ride with me or one of my brothers. I'll pick you up for work every day and make sure you have a ride home."

"I'm not your responsibility, Nate."

Serious blue eyes looked right up at him. While she sat on his lap, looking soft, vulnerable, and desirable. "I think you are. I *want* you to be my responsibility. And not just because of that bastard Gunderson."

"Nate?"

"I'm not going to say it over and over again, Perci. You know I want you. I have for a very, very long time."

"We kept fighting."

"Yes, we did."

"You scared me, Nate. I was dealing with you during the day, and I just didn't know what to do. So I fought."

"I'm sorry that I made things tough for you. I never intended to. You just...scared me, too. And turned me on faster than a damned switch. It took me a while to understand that you didn't realize it. And were younger than I thought. Less experienced."

"I've got more experience than any of my sisters." She frowned. "Well, I did have. I strongly suspect they've made up for it lately."

Nate laughed, even though the subject matter and her position were making him beyond uncomfortable. He put his hands on her thighs and shifted her away from where he really wanted her. "I'm more than willing to help you make up for that."

Perci sobered. "I'm sorry for my part in what happened when we'd fight. It just...seemed easier to *fight* with you than Gunderson. Maybe if I had fought *him,* his son wouldn't have tried to hurt Pip and Matt. Or my cousin Nikki."

Nate pulled her close. "No, honey. It wasn't your fault what Jay did to your sister. Any of it. It's all on *him.* The apple didn't fall far from the tree. Gunderson—either of them—had no right to do what they did. And Clive Gunderson will never hurt or scare you again. No matter what I have to do."

Nate pulled her closer and kissed her.

He repeated that vow silently.

Clive Gunderson would *never* look at her sideways ever again.

He was going to be gentle, unthreatening, despite the fire burning in him. But they both knew exactly what he wanted—what she wanted. Nate's fingers went to the fastener on the back of that blue silk. He parted it quickly.

Perci shivered against him. Nate's body tightened, with hunger. With anticipation.

He had wanted this woman for so long.

Nate had just slipped the silk off her shoulders, when he saw the flash of headlights.

Lights where they shouldn't be. If anyone was on his property, it would have been his brothers. They would have all called first.

"Stay here, honey. Someone's outside." He pulled the blue silk back into place. Hopefully whoever was out there could be dealt with quickly.

He wanted that dress off.

"If you're going outside, Nate, I'm going to be right there with you. You're not shaking me that easily. It's just as likely to be a member of my family as it is yours now, remember?"

Nate swallowed a curse he wrapped his fingers around hers and moved quietly to the window.

A gunshot broke through the night, sending glass shattering around him.

Nate jerked her closer and yanked her into the hall and held her until the sound of tires squealing away split the air.

32

CLIVE KNEW WHAT HE WAS DOING WAS BEYOND stupid. If Masterson or that girl saw him, they'd ruin everything else he had going on.

He had his own future to think about, sick as that made him.

It should be Jay who had years ahead. If anyone had needed to go, it should have been Clive.

No one but Maria and Jay would have mourned his passing.

He pulled his pistol from the glovebox where he'd stashed it before the damned banquet.

All he had to do was aim the damned thing

right at that window and take care of that girl. It would be so easy.

They'd left the light on. He had watched them talk for five minutes.

Watched Masterson slip that dress off her shoulders and show her exactly what he wanted. Clive snorted.

Figured.

Hell, if he hadn't been in a mood he'd be doing the same thing to Maria right now. His phone buzzed and he grabbed for it, almost dropping his damned pistol like a rookie.

Masterson's shadow stepped in front of the window.

Clive acted on instinct. He aimed. And fired.

In the next instant, when he realized what he'd done, he shoved the truck into gear and floored it out of there.

He didn't stop until he'd made it the thirty miles back to Maria's. She opened the door to him quickly. "Clive? Honey?"

He didn't stop to think. He leaned down and kissed her.

Trying to at least *feel* something.

33

Nate was beyond angry. Perci saw it in the controlled way he dealt with his brother and Joel's deputies.

There was glass everywhere. Nate had blood staining the white shirt of his tux. He'd let her have two minutes to check the wounds. She'd pulled glass from his forearm, while trying to get control of herself.

She'd slipped his jacket off his shoulders less than two minutes before the bullet from a .38 had shattered the glass and embedded in the drywall behind them.

It had missed Nate by less than six inches.

Her eyes burned.

She never wanted anything to happen to this man.

Just how she felt for him was kind of hard for her to miss at the moment. It had become crystal to her when they'd been pressed together in the hallway. He had wrapped his body around hers. Protecting. Like always.

But she'd wanted to protect *him*, too. The urge had been just as deep and real and overwhelming as it had been in the moment when that beam had nearly crushed Pip.

Because she loved him.

Joel and his people looked around outside. There weren't any tire tracks. No signs of who it had been.

Joel had found evidence himself of teenagers. Near where the gunshot had come from.

Even homemade targets.

No doubt Nate's brother would be asking every teenager in the county where they'd been tonight. Just how close she'd come to losing him sickened her.

When Joel offered to drive her home, while Nate cleaned up the mess and covered the window, she refused.

No doubt her brother-in-law knew exactly

what had happened before they'd been interrupted.

Perci didn't care. All that mattered to her was that she was right where she was supposed to be. With Nate.

She'd been fighting that long enough.

Perci looked at Joel and Nate, struck again by how perfect they looked. Mastersons were made right; that was for sure. "No, I'm not going anywhere. I'm staying with Nate. No matter what."

34

Nate dug out a spare T-shirt from the boxes he'd already brought to the house. There were some sweats, as well. They'd be way too big, but she'd be covered by more than the dress that had been ripped by glass. He pushed the anger away again. Now wasn't the time.

Not exactly how he had envisioned his evening ending, but they were both safe, and that was what mattered. Perci didn't even have more than a scratch or two on her.

If she had...if he had lost her...

She had the broom and the dustpan when he came back in after speaking with his brother. "I'll sweep up the glass, if you want to get some boards to cover the window tonight. Keep out the rain. We can get this cleaned up in less than an hour, I think."

"Why didn't you leave?" Nate figured they'd beaten around the bush long enough. Too much dancing around each other. Nothing would ever get resolved that way. "Persephone, why did you choose to stay?"

"Well, it wasn't because of pomegranate seeds, that's for sure." She clutched the broom tightly.

He took it from her hand. He didn't care about the damned broom. He let it clatter to the floor.

Hands reached. He wasn't sure who moved first. Then she was in his arms. Right where she belonged.

"I wasn't going to leave you tonight. I told you that." She meant it. Her stomach tightened with nerves. Everything was going to change tonight. They both knew it. And there was no going back "Nate?"

And then he grabbed her by the waistband of the far too big sweatpants and used the cotton to lift her right off of her feet. "Did you mean what we were doing before?"

Perci didn't answer, just nodded.

"Then I say screw this window. The mess. I say we finish what we started, before we both forget how we feel right now. Take a chance for once."

"I've never hated you, Nate. I want you to be clear on that." Perci slipped her arms around his broad shoulders. He still had his hand on her rear, holding her off the ground. He was a full twelve inches taller than she was, and more than one hundred and fifty pounds heavier. Never had she felt the differences between them more. "I'm still trying to figure out exactly what it is that I feel for you. But I don't despise you. Not anymore."

"Good. Because I've burned for you from the very moment we met."

Months. That was more than eighteen months ago. "Nate?"

"My brothers knew. Hell, half the people at the hospital knew. You were the only one who didn't."

Perci was quiet for a moment as he carried her up the stairs. Eighteen months ago, she was in no position to even think about a relationship with a man like Nate Masterson. He had terrified her from the very first meeting. Then the fire and flames had started between them, and that was all she had focused on.

He had scared her on a seriously deep level. So she had run. Figuratively. Run and fought and snarled and done anything she could do to keep him away.

It hadn't worked.

She had fought this man from the moment they'd met until the night his brother had dragged a drunken Phoenix home. Within hours, Nate had been camped on her couch. Watching over her sister.

She'd been terrified that night, too. She'd known how concussions could be, known what a risk Phoebe had taken because they couldn't pay the hospital bill. Having Nate right there *had* made some of that fear more manageable.

But the flames between them had gotten so much worse after that.

Until tonight. It was time to stop trying to extinguish those flames, and just see what happened when the fire ran its course.

And being in his arms felt absolutely right. She slipped her legs around his waist and tightened her arms on his neck. "Do you have a bed here?"

"You'd better believe I do."

Perci leaned down and kissed him. She wasn't going anywhere else tonight. She pulled back and looked at him. "Then take me there. I think we've waited long enough."

35

Rhea knew something had finally happened between Nate and Perci the instant they walked in the front door. The sun was already up, and Perci had that just-loved-look. Nate could barely take his eyes—or his hands—off the girl.

Rhea bit back a secret smile. She was a mother, and she didn't like to even think about her sons' love lives in that way, but she was damned glad Nate had *finally* done something about that girl. Slower than pond scum in a light breeze that boy was.

Anyone with two eyes could see that they belonged together. "Good morning. Did you get the place cleaned up?"

She would just pretend they'd been over there cleaning all night. The way any innocent mother her age would.

"I'll get new windows installed today. After I head in to work for a while." Nate watched the girl as she disappeared down the hall toward the guest room. There was such intensity in his eyes.

Such...love.

Rhea missed her husband more than she had in a long time right then and there. Having her man look at her the way her son was looking at Perci was something she would always miss.

She missed Daniel so much.

Sometimes it hurt to look at the sons they'd created together. Rhea masked her pain from her most perceptive child by hugging him quickly. "I'm glad no one was hurt. Did your brother say who it was yet?"

"Most likely some dumb kid shooting at cans on the outskirts of our property. He found fresh cans out that way. Or drunk and being a little shit. Just got out of hand and took off when they real-ized what they'd done."

Rhea nodded. It wouldn't have been the first time.

The Mastersons had long owned parts of the

county that were extremely remote. Even her own sons had done such stupid stuff when they'd all been teens. Levi especially had given them fits. Daniel had thought that boy would never outgrow it. Then at nineteen Levi had gotten a job at a neighboring ranch, saved his money up, and bought five acres near where they were now. To raise beef cattle. After that, Daniel had taken their youngest son on as a full partner in the Masterson ranch holdings. Said Levi was going to put his brain to work for Mastersons and no one else. Which was exactly what Levi had always wanted. Without a single protest from his older brothers. Her boys had always known their ways in life. And gone after them. "I'm just thankful you and Perci are safe."

His gaze immediately went toward the hall-way. Like a magnet.

Rhea smiled to herself. Once her son finally made up his mind what he wanted to do about that girl that was when things would finally settle. Would finally be the way they were supposed to. In the meantime, she had some friends at CPS to talk with.

If Nate didn't do something about that child needing a home, Rhea would take care of it herself.

That little one was meant to be her granddaughter, and Rhea wasn't about to let Ivy go, either.

Things were going to work out for Nate, Perci, and Ivy exactly the way they were supposed to. Rhea was going to make certain of it.

36

Her sister's coppery red-blond hair shone in the sun when Pan climbed out of Levi's truck. Perci stayed where she was, keeping the swing in slow rhythm. Ivy had missed her last night. The toddler hadn't wanted to let go of Perci once she'd walked in the door. Perci had barely been able to change out of her borrowed clothes.

Now Ivy snuggled close and slept the limp sleep of the innocent.

Pan paused just on the first step. "Well. *You're* still here. Did the devil give you pomegranates or something?"

"Something like that." The original myth said Hades had fed Persephone fruit to trick her into staying with him. Perci was starting to suspect it had been something much more binding than fruit. Her arms tightened around the child. She suspected the devil had given that long ago namesake heat...and love.

That was the reason the original Persephone had stayed.

Even if it was just in a myth.

Now that Pan was back it was almost time to turn Ivy over.

If Pan and Levi were willing.

A child was a huge responsibility.

It wasn't quite fair of them to ask Pan to take responsibility for another child when her sister had spent the last two years worrying about finding the money to feed three others.

But that was just another excuse.

Perci didn't want to let Ivy go just yet. Even to her own sister.

"Let me see her. Phoebe emailed me and said she's absolutely adorable, *Mama Perci.*" There was a look in Pan's eyes that had Perci mentally squirming. They'd talk later, she had no doubt about it.

Perci had some questions of her own. Was Pan prepared to take on responsibility for Ivy right now? Pan had just gotten married, just experienced a horrible ordeal, and was only twenty-two—though Pan would be twenty-three soon—and a child was a big commitment. A lifetime one.

But if not Pan, then what would happen to Ivy? Joel and Phoebe, perhaps? Phoebe would make an excellent mother.

As would Pip. Her twin *would* be a mother in a little less than seven months. Was it fair to ask Pip to take on a traumatized almost three-year-old, as well?

She wished. But there was no way Perci would ever get approved as a placement for Ivy. It was going to have to be Pan or Phoebe. She'd just become Ivy's favorite aunt, or something. She'd be there to help whichever sister became Ivy's mother, however she could.

It would work out the way it was supposed to. She had to have faith in that.

But the thought of not being with Ivy every single day, of not making sure she was safe and healthy and loved—even though the rational part of her knew her sister would do just fine—hurt her.

Pan and Levi carried their luggage inside. Perci continued to rock the porch swing gently.

Until a big shadow passed in front of her. She paused.

Nate settled himself on the swing next to her. "Coming inside soon? I don't want you to get cold out here."

"We're fine." She was going to hold Ivy as long as she could. Stupid of her, maybe, but Perci knew the time would come when she'd have to *stop* being Mama Perci and let someone else be Ivy's mother for real. The little girl deserved it.

But that didn't make Perci feel any better equipped to let the child go. Just not yet.

She wasn't supposed to fall for the child as quickly as she had. It was always supposed to be temporary.

Just like falling for Nate hadn't been in the plan, either.

But she could no longer deny the devil. He had become her world just as fast as Ivy had.

"Are you?" His arm slipped around her shoulder and he scooted her closer. Perci let her head rest against his broad chest. He smelled perfect, all man and spice and outside.

It was so much nicer when they weren't fighting against each other so badly. "I honestly don't know."

"Because of last night?"

She smiled. So the Great Nate had his doubts? She never would have guessed it. "No. Not because of last night. Because of Ivy. Is it fair to ask Pan to take on a traumatized toddler? She's already had to do so much for *our* family. She gave up her dreams of going away to college for the rest of us. Now, I don't know that asking her to take on a child is right. Shouldn't she just be free to enjoy Levi for a little while without all the worry that goes with a kid?"

"Maybe. But things rarely happen in a fair way. We both know that." He reached over her with his free hand and adjusted the blanket covering Ivy's shoulder. His touch lingered on the little girl's mussed blond hair. Perci loved watching the two of them together. "We have to think about what's best for Ivy."

"And if Pan and Levi don't take her, chances are good she'll be sent someplace else in the state." And they would never see her again. Perci knew it in her gut. "And she'll just be gone. Like she was never here."

"Yes."

"I..."

"I'll speak to my brothers. Levi first, since she's

already here with him, technically. If he and Pan can't, I have two more brothers, and you have two more sisters. They'll all make damned good parents; we'll make sure we don't lose her, honey. I can promise you that. Hopefully between my brothers and my mother, we have enough pull in the community to finally do some good. I won't give up."

Perci closed her eyes. In that moment, she believed him.

Trusted him to do just that.

They rocked until she drifted off to sleep with him holding her and her holding Ivy. Just like that was exactly where they all belonged.

37

Rhea didn't mean to be intimidating with her new daughters-in-law. She didn't think a one of them were pushovers. They couldn't be and have captured her boys' attention. This youngest one was a shrewd little bright-eyed cookie. Sharp as a tack, she'd heard. Very, very pretty, too.

All of her daughters-in-law—and her future daughter-in-law, once Nate got on the ball—were beyond beautiful girls. Beautiful, smart, loyal, and just wonderful. Rhea couldn't have found a better crop of girls for her sons if she'd tried.

Which technically she had, at least with Nate. Which had no doubt precipitated it all.

Pandora stood at the window, watching her sister.

"They are really doing a fine job, taking care of that baby the way they have," Rhea said. She knew what the plan was for Ivy. *This* girl, instead of the other. Rhea was fine with that, but any fool could see that Perci was the best mother for *Ivy*. Her sisters would just be second-best. Rhea stepped up next to her youngest daughter-in-law and put a hand on the shorter woman's shoulder. "They don't even realize how they look."

"Oh?" There was a wariness in the girl's blue eyes. One Rhea didn't understand until she recalled what Joel had told her had happened to these girls.

Damn that old rat Clive Gunderson for daring to torture those children the way he had. If she had any influence in this town at all, she'd make it clear that he wasn't to go near her girls again. It would take some doing and some thinking and calling in a few favors, but Rhea would manage that while her boys did what they had to in order for their wives to feel safe in Masterson County again.

"How beautiful. They both really love that little girl. I'm glad they were there to help her."

Pan nodded. "Perci will help anyone who

needs it. No matter what. It's why she became a nurse."

Rhea nodded. She'd suspected as much. There was a gentleness underneath the fire. She'd noticed that right off.

Had Nate?

"Can I ask you a question?" Pan asked. "How long have she and Nate been like that?"

Rhea looked through the glass. All she could see was the side of her son on the swing. The front porch was a wraparound, and the swing was at a corner angle. But she knew what Pan meant. They looked like they'd been wrapped up in each other's arms forever.

She *knew* something had happened between them last night. A mother wasn't stupid, no matter that they claimed they'd been up all night cleaning broken glass out of Nate's floor. "They've been circling each other for a few days, but they came home this morning like that. Eyes only for each other. And Ivy."

Pan's expression tightened. "Perci loves that little girl."

"Very much so."

"What's going to happen to Ivy?"

"For now, Nate's officially the foster parent on

record. But the social workers could move her at any time if they find a different home for her. I've made a few calls. She should be secure here, but... at her age, they'll want to get her into a permanent home as quickly as possible." She suspected what was going to happen, of course, but how did this girl feel about almost instant mommyhood? "Levi's also a registered foster parent. But to keep her here, you'd have to do the training as well."

Her eyes widened, then she looked at her sister. There was a world of emotions in those blue eyes. Determination, love, hope. Resolution. Her shoulders stiffened. "If that's what it takes, then of course."

Rhea already had a pretty high opinion of her daughters-in-law, but felt it get higher for this one in that moment. Tylers took *family* very seriously. She smiled. "You are very much like your mother, aren't you?"

"You knew her?"

"Sweetie, I delivered you and your sisters. Not your brothers, but each one of you girls. Perci and Pip were the most difficult. I also babysat your mother and aunt when they were girls. I loved them both quite a bit."

"I didn't know that. My aunt...she left with her

husband almost fifteen years ago, when she was my age. We haven't seen or heard from her since. We don't even know if *she* knows about my mother."

The pain was there, in the blue eyes, of a child missing a parent. It was a pain Rhea knew. It was a pain her sons all knew. And her daughters-in-law.

"I'm sorry. I'm sure Robin had her reasons." She'd grown into a wild girl who looked very much like the one curled up with Nate on the swing, but Robin had had a good heart. "Maybe she'll come back some day. Come, you and I will have a talk."

"About?"

"What we can do for those three out there on the porch. I think you and I may have similar ideas about just what needs to happen for Ivy."

Pan's smile was practically blinding. "You really are just like your son, aren't you?"

Rhea shot her a mild smile of her own. "Which one are you referring to? *Nate* is very much like his father, stubborn old goat."

She had her suspicions. Her Levi was just as much a planner and schemer as his mother.

Pan just laughed. "You know exactly who I mean."

"I most certainly do." Levi's pretty little wife knew exactly what her youngest son was like.

Yes, she couldn't have picked a better love for Levi, even if she'd had the chance. Fate, or God above, however someone wanted to think about it, had done right by her youngest boy.

Now it was time for Rhea to see that it did right by her third son, too.

38

JUDE KNEW IT WAS A MISTAKE THE INSTANT she looked at Pandora Masterson. Not that the woman was off-putting and or a bad risk.

It was just that Pandora was not Perci. Nate and Perci were the best fit for little Ivy.

Jude and Rhea Masterson had both agreed on that when Rhea had stopped by her office and made a lunch date with Jude's boss. But Levi and his wife were definitely more than a good choice for second-best. Ivy wouldn't have to leave the house she'd become accustomed to. Or the routine she was learning. Phoebe Masterson would still watch her during the day. She'd still have frequent access to Perci, the woman she obviously adored.

Even Nate Masterson would be a regular fixture in the little girl's life. The little girl wouldn't have to make *any* major changes at all. She couldn't ask for a better relocation plan.

But it still didn't quite feel right to Jude. She looked at the tall man beside her. "Dr. Masterson, as her legal foster parent, you get the first option. If you'd like to pursue adoption, you have a strong shot of winning, from what I've seen so far."

He hesitated.

His attention shifted to the woman and child in the next room. He watched them for the longest time. When he looked back at Jude, there were conflicting emotions on his handsome face. "Ivy needs, deserves a mother. A father who can be there more than I can be. Levi and Pan, hell, any of my brothers and their wives, would be a better choice for her."

"I'm not so sure of that. She loves you. And she's bonded *with you.* You and Perci."

"I know. But I'm not so sure we're—I'm—in a position to be a good fit for her right now."

"I think you're in a great position. I'll tell you what. I'll hold off on filing my recommendation papers for a few weeks. I'm about to go on vacation. It can wait. In the meantime, will you consider it?"

Jude didn't know why she was pushing for this so hard. It wasn't like the girl would even have to move out of the house she was living in. She'd just call a different Masterson *daddy*.

Nate and Perci and that little girl were becoming a family, almost right in front of her eyes. A miracle.

Jude didn't get to see many of those any more. It was one heck of an incentive to keep pushing.

Perci and Nate were what was best for Ivy.

And that was all Jude was truly after, after all.

What was best for Ivy.

39

THE DISCUSSION WASN'T GOING THE WAY NATE had wanted.

His brother was looking at him like he was crazy. Nate had always hated when Levi looked at him just like that. And no doubt his brother knew it.

"Let me get this straight. You want us to take Ivy?" Levi asked, slowly. "Permanently. Not just like for a week or so? Like you said originally—which was the perfect excuse for me to get Pan away from that idiot Bowles and Hunter L. Clark, himself."

"That's what I said," Nate said, ignoring the references to the director and his top actor. "I don't want to see her go into foster care permanently. The list of adoptive families in this area is slim. She needs a stable, loving home. One with people I can trust. That Perci can trust. The two are... bonded. I don't want to break that. I think it should be you and Pan who take her."

"I don't know if you've missed it, since you're the dumbest of us all—but you live here, too. How is that going to be a better change for her if we're the legal guardians of the kid or not? To be honest, we just got married. I was kind of hoping to kick you out and have some naked-in-the-kitchen-with-the-housekeeper time. Not deal with snot faces. Not that Ivy isn't a great kid, but I'd have to do some serious thinking about this. And talk to Pandora. She'd be the one responsible for the day-to-day care of Ivy. We were planning on kids. But in a few years, maybe."

Nate nodded. He had expected as much. His brother might be a bit of a clown at times—Levi had constant good humor, it seemed—but his brother was an extremely responsible man.

He wouldn't just keep a kid because she was there. Levi would make damned sure he was the best fit for that child.

Levi and Pan would make wonderful parents for Ivy.

The best he could imagine.

Other than Perci, that was.

She and Ivy just seemed to fit together.

At least if her sister adopted the little girl, Perci would still get to maintain that relationship. It wouldn't be the most perfect relationship setup, but she'd still get to be a huge part of Ivy's life. Nate wanted that for the both of them.

"Just think about it. The kid needs a good place to grow up. I can't think of a better place than right here."

"I can." Levi's own gaze was on the kid in the front yard, watched over by the two beautiful redheads.

"Oh?"

"It's easy, bro. The kid belongs with you. You... and the woman she already calls *mama*. I think you need to go grab your girl and do what you got to do to make it a permanent thing. For her, you, and the kid. Can't think of a better solution. Just do it, Nate. Fix this so you all three get what you want. We both know you're capable of it."

40

LEVI'S WORDS RATTLED IN NATE'S HEAD LONG after he'd left the house he'd shared with his brother for the last few years. They had started there, in the home they'd grown up in, but Levi had expanded the original ranch to include four others, including their grandfather's old place.

But Nate had wanted that house.

For the past year, he'd been fixing it up himself in his spare time. It relaxed him. And made it more *his* than any other place he had ever lived.

It was finally finished. Ready for him to move in and claim it.

For the first time, the idea of doing that didn't sit well with him.

Not without her.

Or Ivy.

Levi's words had struck something in him, and he knew it. Made it feel *right*.

Like it was meant to.

Gave him ideas he didn't have any business having.

Nate sat next to Perci and Ivy at the dinner table. Perci kept an eye on the little girl constantly. She'd make a damned fine mother someday. It wasn't the first time he'd thought that. She might breathe fire where he was concerned, but she had a streak of compassion three miles wide.

He wanted to see her holding *his* child someday. And someday real soon.

She must have felt him staring. She shot him a pointed look and smirked. "Hungry?"

Hell yes, he was. For her. For everything.

"I'm moving out." He said it to her first. Her shock was almost immediate. Her...fear and mistrust. Nate leaned forward abruptly. He never wanted this woman to look at him like that ever again.

"I'm sorry? Where to?"

"The homestead's finished, isn't it?" Levi

asked, sending him a far-too-knowing look. Damned calculating idiot.

"Yes. The new windows are installed. The last of the flooring is laid. I can move in at any time." *They* could move in at any time.

He just had to get her there and get her to agree to say *yes*. Yes, to everything he had planned.

He looked at Ivy as she reached for Perci. Perci scooped her up automatically, and Nate got exactly what he'd wished for her.

The woman he loved, holding the child he was now considering *his*. It didn't get more perfect than that.

"Not yet?" Perci's eyes were wide. Soft. A little surprised. Nate's gut tightened. "Not until Ivy's settled?"

"I can wait. Been here this long." He found himself nodding. He wasn't ready to leave either one of them. "It just seems silly to leave the house empty over there when it's ready."

"But it's not silly," his mother said, pointedly. "It's for Ivy."

Perci's eyes stared into his, and that's when he knew.

He wasn't leaving this house without *her*. Or the little girl right next to her. He stood abruptly.

He had some calls to make. "I need to take care of a few things. It'll take maybe an hour in my office. After that, I'll be out to help you get her ready for bed. It's my turn to read to her tonight, sweetheart. Then you and I are going to...talk."

Nate leaned down and brushed a kiss against her lips, deliberately. Perci's eyes widened, but she didn't pull away.

He deepened the kiss, just enough to make his point.

Staking *his* claim. No doubt it would go through the family grapevine like wildfire.

When he looked up, Levi's eyes were laughing at him. But knowing. His younger brother just *got* it.

Nate smirked. He had some plans to make to keep Perci right where she was.

41

PERCI TICKLED IVY'S BELLY, MAKING THE little girl laugh. Pan was in the chair next to the bed, telling her all about what had happened between Rowland Bowles and his assistant. Perci listened to her sister with half an ear while she finished dressing Ivy.

"So tell me, you and Nate. All the details."

"Like you shared with you and Levi?" Perci sent her sister a mild look. She'd barely known Levi and Pan had gotten together until a jealous neighbor had nearly killed Pan. "There are some things we are not going to talk about."

"Uh-huh. You told me about your first time."

"No. I told *Pip*. You were listening through the

vent in the attic. Perv." She'd been eighteen and so sure he was the greatest thing since chocolate. That had lasted about six months until he went away on a baseball scholarship and she hit the community college's nursing program eighty miles away. She'd already known what she was going to do, and his plans had taken him far from Masterson County. She barely remembered what he looked like now.

Or the other men she'd dated since then, even though she'd not been serious enough about any of them to go to bed with them.

All she could see in her mind was green eyes and warm brown hair and a man intent on loving *her* well into the night.

"Hey, how else was I going to learn? You, Pip, and Phoebe barely told me anything good back then."

"I spent the night with him. You know that. Everyone knows that."

"He lured you to his underworld and kept you all night. You know what that means, right?"

"That it is none of your business?" She pulled *Cat in the Hat* pajamas over small feet, then slipped the shirt over Ivy's head. "Nate and I...I don't know. I'm sure you'll have a front-row seat when I figure it out."

She *had* figured it out. She just wasn't about to tell her younger sister that before she told the man in question.

Perci had to also face the fact that Nate could feel completely different, too. There was nothing written in stone after what they had done. To him, it could be far more casual than it was to her.

Someone knocked on the door lightly. She turned.

There Nate was, his brother at his shoulder.

"I'm looking for my wife." Levi held out a hand to Pan and pulled her from the chair. He whispered something in her ear that had Pan's cheeks flushing. Then he grinned at Perci. "I'm taking her for a moonlight...stroll...around the backyard."

"It's getting cold out." Perci felt obligated to point out. Truth was, she wanted them both gone.

"I'll keep her warm. Be back in a bit."

Then they were gone.

Nate settled onto the bed next to Ivy. Perci adjusted the covers. Nate read softly and evenly, Ivy snuggled against him. Within fifteen minutes, Ivy was out. Then it was just the two of them.

42

He didn't waste a moment. The instant she had settled Ivy into the pillow and tucked the blankets back around the now sleeping child, Nate grabbed her by the hand.

His room was right next door. He dragged her there quickly. He closed the door and then had her up against it. His mouth covered hers. Her hands went to the buttons of his shirt.

Perci had clever little fingers. He'd learned that the night before. "Honey, I don't want you to leave."

She stilled against him. "What do you mean?"

He cursed himself inside his head. He should

have kept his mouth shut. Until after. "I don't want you to leave *here*. Correction. When I go to the new place, I want you to go with me. You and Ivy. Come with me."

Tyler blue eyes widened. "For how long?"

Forever. "You know what I mean."

Her fingers paused. "No, I don't. I don't know what any of this means. *This* changes everything."

"Yes." The way things were supposed to be. He *should* have been with her long before Joel and Phoebe had met. If he hadn't fought so hard a year and a half ago everything would have happened so much faster. Maybe. Or maybe not. Maybe they had all had to go through what they had to find what they had now.

That thought didn't even make sense to him.

"I...just can't decide to move in with you. I have my family to think about. And...we've fought so much. What makes you think we won't start doing that again once this newness wears off?"

"We'll fight. But making up is going to be a hell of a lot more fun." Nate brushed his lips against her neck, then scooped her up. Her legs wrapped around his waist. Nate carried her to his bed and put her right where he had wanted her for a very,

very long time. "And your family will be fine. There will be a few changes. Maybe your dad has to get some help in during the evenings. But it'll work out. You'll be with me. Where you belong. Say yes, Persephone. Move in with me. We'll figure everything else out later."

43

SHE'D KNOWN SHE LOVED HIM FROM THE moment she had realized she trusted him in a way she hadn't trusted a man before. Maybe as early as the night they'd treated Ivy. But the idea of changing *everything* about her life like this terrified her. She'd clung so tightly to her family over the last few years that she didn't know if she could even think about letting go just yet. "I don't know."

Perci looked up at him, honestly expecting to see anger in his green eyes. There was none there. Just understanding. And hope. It was the hope that got to her.

"I want you here. However I can get you. But I'll wait if I have to. I get why you're afraid. I'm going to be here whenever you're ready. No rush. We've waited this long. We can take our time— unlike the rest of our crazy siblings."

Tears hit her eyes. She nodded. Perci wrapped her arms around his shoulders and pulled him closer. "Thank you. My family—"

"Means everything to you. I know. I have since Joel walked in the ER carrying Phoebe in his arms. That night...I lay on your couch and dreamed of you. The idea that you were just down the hall had me...unable to sleep much at all. If you hadn't been sharing with Pip...hell, I may have snuck in there and just carried you off. It wasn't the first time I'd had that thought. Only...I knew what you slept in after that night. The things I imagined after that were a lot more...accurate." Nate's hand slipped down over the buttons on her flannel shirt. One by one, he opened the cotton until she was laying there in front of him with nothing but her bra showing. "I have dreamed of having you in here a thousand times."

"We've only known each other a little over a year. You must have a very active sleep cycle."

"You're in and out of my dreams every hour all night long, it seems." The shirt was gone, then the bra followed. Perci just let him. For a little while.

Then it would be her turn to get him how she wanted *him*.

It didn't matter that his brother and her sister would be in the room down the hall soon. None of it mattered.

Just being with him. Holding each other.

He wasn't pushing her or pressuring her or trying to take charge. He was just *there*. Waiting.

The decision was hers.

But that was for tomorrow. Tonight was for *them*. Perci leaned closer and kissed him.

44

NATE WAS CALLED IN TO THE HOSPITAL EARLY the next day. They'd had the day off and were planning to spend it with Ivy, taking her shopping for some more child appropriate furniture. Pan had intended to go with her, but her sister had called off at the last minute, claiming one of her infrequent migraines.

Perci suspected Pan had never *had* migraines; her sister was smart enough to use the excuse when she was up to something.

Conniving little brat. Pan had always been one.

Perci took the credit card Nate had given her and drove into Masterson. There was a lovely little shop on Main Street that she'd never been able to shop at before. But Nate had told her to get the best for Ivy.

For *his* house.

She hadn't missed the whimsical pink bedroom right across the hall from the master suite. It was the kind every little girl dreamed about.

"Mama Perci, me hungry. Again."

She looked in the rearview mirror at the child. Ivy had a hopeful look on her beautiful little face.

"Food first? We'll go to the diner. Get a hamburger and French fries."

"Yum. Ivy likes hamburgers."

45

Rhea had just placed her order—she really should *not* love those onion rings as much as she did—when the front doors opened and her sweet little almost grandbaby came in. It took Rhea a moment to figure out which twin it was, but chances were good the woman with Ivy was Perci.

She looked back at the diner's second generation owner. "Theirs is on me, too."

"Of course. That's a pretty little thing there."

She'd known the woman behind the counter since they were girls together. Florence should have long retired by now, but she was a stubborn one. Her business was her life—her business and the daughter and granddaughter who now helped her run it.

Rhea understood. The hospital had been her purpose, too.

That, and raising those boys of hers with Daniel.

"That's my new grandbaby, Flo." Rhea had already snapped half a dozen pictures of Ivy to share with her closest friends when she saw them.

"Heard that may be your new daughter-in-law soon, too."

"Oh, I'm planning to make sure that happens. She's a real sweetheart. Just like her sisters." Perci might be a bit sassier than her sisters, but Rhea thought that was just the child's way of hiding more insecurities than Perci wanted to admit to.

"They always were good girls. Shame what happened to their mama. And everything that's happened since. They deserve a bit of a good break now. Saw the way that last boy of yours was eying her the other day. He's a handful, I bet."

"Perci can handle him. I have no doubt about that."

She waited until Perci was closer. "Hi, honey. Ivy, come give Nana a hug and a kiss."

"Nana, hug." Ivy reached those little arms out

to her, and Rhea took her. She smelled like clean baby and apple juice. A rush of love went through her. She'd spoken with Levi just that morning. He and Pan were ready and willing to do what they had to for this little one, too.

Or they had been until Nate had spoken with them both that morning while Perci had still been sleeping.

She smiled, thrilled to her toes at how wonderful her sons were.

Nate was going to move forward with adopting Ivy, as soon as she was freed for adoption. In the meantime, the little one was staying right where she was.

Becoming a Masterson.

It wasn't how she'd expected to get her first grandbaby, but to Rhea it was perfect. Ivy was the grandchild of her heart. And she always would be. "There's my baby girl. What are you doing today?"

"Mama Perci and Ivy go to the store. Then Pee-be."

The bruises were fading. The girl's eyes were brighter than they had been. The little pink top and white shorts were clean and neat. She was happy. The way a child should be. Rhea looked at Perci. "Where's that son of mine?"

"Nate was called in to the hospital. He'll be there most of the day, I think."

Perci was still wary with her, but Rhea had her measure. That hiss and fire was used to hide the fear. She'd asked Levi point blank what had happened to their girls, and the stories he had told her had sickened her. To think that family had dealt with all of it alone like that.

It shouldn't have been that way. Damn that Clive Gunderson for not being the man a sheriff should be.

Her son was a much better sheriff, hands down. And that wasn't just mother pride talking. The way that Gunderson had abused his power—she wished there was a way to make that man pay for what he'd done to her girls.

She suspected this one was the one who needed to *heal* the most, even though Perci undoubtedly hid how hurt she actually was.

Levi had told her enough to raise her hair, hinting that what happened to Perci still remained a mystery.

Rhea resisted the urge to just hug her and tell her that her world was going to be a better place now. That Nate would fix everything he possibly could.

Hopefully Nate understood that as well. "And you and Miss Ivy?"

"We're furniture shopping. We're going to pick it out today and Nate's going to swing by and pick it up on his way home." Perci took Ivy back when the toddler reached for her. She quickly ordered, then looked at Rhea when the cashier told her the bill was on Rhea.

"It's the least I can do for my new grandbaby." *And* Ivy's new mama. But Rhea kept that part to herself. Best not to rush things. Yet. Strategy was as much about *timing* as it was action. "Sit with me. Make me look like I'm not up to no good today."

Perci smiled.

Such a beautiful girl. She and Nate would make beautiful, beautiful babies. Rhea bit back a smile, as she imagined it. All of her grandchildren would most likely look very similar. Rhea loved genetics. All the possibilities. She couldn't wait to see how alike and how different those precious little ones would be. Seven more months and Pip and Matt would take care of the beginning of that for her.

She'd just focus on Ivy first. Give Nate and

Perci a bit more time to make her third grandbaby on their own before she started pushing.

Pip and Matt and their future little one were enough to keep her busy for now. And Ivy.

"Come. Talk to this crazy old lady, Miss Ivy. Tell Nana all about Mama Perci and Daddy Nate."

It sounded so perfect. She couldn't have planned it any better.

46

Rhea Masterson was such a blend of each of her sons, with her own unique dose of snark and humor, that Perci found herself relaxing as the lunch went on. She had *not* planned to eat lunch with Nate's mother, but the woman had plenty of stories to tell on her sons. Not just Nate. Some of the things his brothers had gotten up to were...hair-raising. Especially Matt. The quietest Masterson brother had been a bit of a daredevil as a kid. The slightly younger Nate had had to rescue Matt more than a few times.

Not to mention what had to be done with Levi. According to Rhea, the only reason Levi had survived his childhood was because Nate had made a point to keep his brother in check.

Apparently Nate was the savior of the group. Always watching, protecting. And slow as molasses sometimes. Rhea made a point of illustrating that particular fact.

Perci knew what the woman was doing, and she could have told her to save her energy. She didn't need to *sell* Perci on Nate any longer. He'd done that all by himself.

She smiled, thinking of what it had been like snuggled in his arms all night.

Pan had sure enjoyed teasing her that morning when Perci had come out of Nate's room and run into her youngest sister in the hall.

It didn't matter. She had been right where she was supposed to be.

But if she was ready to make that a permanent thing, she wasn't quite sure yet.

She needed to return to her *real* life and make her decision. Soon.

Without Nate and Ivy there with her—distracting her. Tempting her with promises of what could be.

She had a lot to think about.

Before she knew it, she was shopping for furniture with Nate's mother. They'd spent a couple of hours before Perci even realized it. And far more of Nate's money than she wanted to think about. When they were finished, Ivy was napping in Rhea's arms, and Perci was exhausted.

Ivy had needed almost everything, including a few more weather-appropriate outfits. And toys. She had only the few Phoebe had packed up from the boys' stashes.

Rhea encouraged them to pick out far more things than a child Ivy's age really needed. But they all enjoyed it.

Nate was probably going to freak when he got his credit card bill, though.

"Honey, go home. I'll take this little one out to your daddy's. I can visit with those little brothers of yours. Catch up with your daddy. You look like you barely slept a wink."

Perci hid a wince.

She *hadn't* slept a wink. And she wasn't about to tell the woman looking at her *why*.

She and Nate had definitely made up for all the nights they *could* have been together if they hadn't been fighting each other so much. She was sore and tired in a way that was absolutely delicious when she thought about it.

Perci wasn't about to tell the man's mother that, though.

But she wouldn't trade even a minute of it. Nate had held her through the night.

For the first time in weeks, months—years—she hadn't had the nightmares. His arms around her had felt right. Perfect. And she wouldn't change a moment.

She wanted more of those moments. She didn't want to waste another night without him.

Resolve filled her when she thought of *not* spending every night with him that she could.

She couldn't do it. She couldn't return to her father's house and her narrow twin bed again. It was time to step off the edge and actively go after what she wanted, what she needed.

And what she needed was Nate.

"I think I'll take you up on that." And grab her things. There were some boxes or totes somewhere. She'd pack them up. Take them to Nate's. He'd issued the invitation.

He wasn't about to stop her now.

She pulled in a breath, as her decision settled around her shoulders. She was going to go home. To her father's. Just long enough to gather her things and...then she was going to find Nate.

She didn't have much. A house as full as theirs had once been didn't leave much space for a lot of personal belongings per person. It wouldn't take long to get everything she'd collected to this point.

And be ready to go with him tonight.

A thrill of anticipation went through her.

She'd be with him tonight.

They could assemble Ivy's furniture together, get her room ready for her, and tuck Ivy into *her* bed tonight.

And then she and Nate could figure out what the future held for all of them.

Together.

47

CLIVE SAT IN THE BACK BOOTH OF THE DINER and watched that girl long past the time he should have left. She was beautiful today. Sun slipped through the window and made that red-brown hair of hers look almost like mahogany silk. She had it braided down her back. It was a bit shorter than it used to be. He'd always thought her hair was a pretty color.

That baby girl was with her again, and he watched. Perci was a natural with the child. Beautiful and easy with the girl in ways Clive hadn't been with Jay and Clint. Hell, he'd barely spent more than an hour or two each day with Jay when he'd been that age and even less than that with Clint.

But this child, she was now the golden angel of the Masterson clan, no doubt. That was Masterson's mother right there, doting on that girl as if she was her real grandbaby.

He didn't even do that with Clint's baby, and she was his great-niece *and* stepgrandbaby. He snorted.

That girl would be given every damned thing she wanted. She'd have a mama who loved her. Not to mention one of the richest men in the county for her daddy. She wouldn't have to want for anything, not like his Jay had. And Clive had had a good job. It just hadn't been enough.

It had eaten into his time with his boy and Clint. He would never forget how much time he'd lost with Jay because of that job that Masterson had taken from him.

Clive adjusted the tie around his neck to keep from choking to death, just as Rhea Masterson scooped the kid up and grabbed the bag from Perci. It was obvious they were moving on from the diner.

He didn't know what else to do.

Clive tossed his trash in the basin nearby. And followed them.

48

CLIVE MUST HAVE SAT IN HIS TRUCK OUTSIDE that damned diner for hours. In the heat. People stared at him like he was a fool, but he didn't give a damn.

None of it mattered. None of it.

He'd lost Jay. And after that shit with that doctor's window, he'd lost Maria. She'd stayed with him for the funeral, but Clive knew the truth.

The only person in this world he gave two shits for anymore wanted nothing else to do with him.

The way Maria had looked at him. With disgust and mistrust.

He'd disappointed her. He hadn't known how she'd felt mattered quite that much to him.

Nothing. He had nothing. Just how empty and cold his future was going to be yawned in front of him.

People walked behind his tailgate.

He noticed the red hair first.

It took him a moment to figure out which one she was.

Her twin wasn't seen much in town, except in the company of that vet husband of hers.

Perci was right there. Right there. Again. Laughing. Holding that child as if she was the most precious gift in the world. Right there. Almost within spitting distance.

Clive forced himself to breathe. To not do something completely stupid.

Perci passed the child to Masterson's mother, then leaned down to put her shopping bags in the trunk of that damned red car of hers.

When she turned, the setting sun caught in her hair and highlighted the red. Made her skin glow.

She looked so damned beautiful, happy, and *alive*.

He could see why Jay had been captivated by the woman who looked just like her.

Alive. She was so damned *alive*.

He wanted to feel that life. Just for a moment.

Clive opened the door and stepped out of the truck.

His suit clung to him, sweat-drenched and bunched. He didn't give a damn. He needed that *life*.

To see something that was real, something other than the sight of his only son in a damned box about to be lowered into the Wyoming ground forever. He had to get that image out of his head.

There had to be something about this girl that it made sense that she'd lived and his son hadn't. There had to be some *reason*.

He stepped out from behind the bed of his truck and right into her path. *"Perci."*

49

At first she didn't recognize the man in front of her. He was dirty, his hair stuck out all over his head. It took her a moment to realize it was sweat. Clive Gunderson's brown eyes were red-rimmed with tears. "Perci."

He just stood there, repeating her name. Staring. At her, at Rhea and Ivy directly behind her.

"Mama, Mama, Mama." Ivy chose that moment to call for her. To remind her that she wasn't alone. Wasn't alone and vulnerable alongside a deserted highway any longer.

Perci stepped to the left, putting herself bodily between Clive Gunderson and Ivy. "Gunderson."

"He's dead."

"I know. Nate told me."

"You're not. You're right here in front of me. Perfect. You're not sorry at all, are you?"

"Why should I be? He almost killed me. He almost killed my sister. And he...*you*...made our family miserable, terrified, for four years. That's hard to forget." All the times he'd terrified her at night coalesced in her mind. Reminding her of everything. Everything she'd lost, everything that had happened to the ones she loved because of it. Everything. Perci wouldn't let him do it to her again. Not anymore. He didn't have power over her anymore. "If you don't mind, we need to get going. It's getting late and Ivy needs dinner and put to bed."

"You'll have it all." He stared at her. Rhea said her name and wrapped one hand around Perci's elbow. "You'll have that baby. Have that doctor. That family of yours. His. You've won. I have nothing. Not now. It's all gone."

Perci risked a glance at Nate's mother. Rhea held Ivy tight. But they were all far too exposed.

And Clive Gunderson held a pistol in his hand. "*Rhea*, get Ivy into the car. Or take her back inside. I think...she needs her diaper changed. Can you take her back inside for me, please? I'll be in to get her in a minute."

50

For the first time in a long while, Rhea didn't know what to do. Her arms tightened around Ivy. Perci shifted in front of her, using her body to protect the little one's.

Clive Gunderson just stood there. Staring. When she saw the gun, Rhea gasped.

His hand was clenching and unclenching on the grip. His eyes were trained on Perci like she was the only one in his world. Fixated. Mad.

She'd seen men like him before.

"Rhea, take Ivy inside. Please?" Perci said again.

Rhea took a step back. She didn't want to leave Perci out there alone. Not with him.

Ivy sniffled and laid her head on Rhea's shoulder. That baby didn't need to be out there for whatever Gunderson was wanting.

"Go, Rhea. *Please.*" The desperation in Perci's words broke through her paralysis.

Rhea understood. She was a mama, too, after all.

"I'll wait for you inside." Rhea took a step away, then another. "Don't take too long, ok?"

"I won't." Perci didn't look at her. Didn't take her eyes off Clive Gunderson.

"Perci," Gunderson said again. "I...tell me *why.*"

"Why what, Gunderson? I don't think you and I have anything to talk about. Not anymore."

Rhea kept going until she reached the sidewalk. She carried the baby inside and grabbed her phone.

She dialed 911 as fast as she could.

51

PERCI STAYED RIGHT WHERE SHE WAS UNTIL she was certain Rhea had had time to get Ivy inside. Then she moved closer to Pan's SUV. "I don't know what you expect me to say. What your son did was wrong. It led to his death, nothing I did. Or my family. He did it. I don't know what you want from me."

Her eyes never left the gun in his hand. She wanted to run. To get as far away from him as possible.

Every single time he'd pulled her over at night, he'd had that same pistol in his hand. He'd forced her to cooperate while he searched her car. While he made her kneel in the mud on four separate occasions.

While he kept her there next to the road while he'd eaten a damned sub sandwich once. She'd despised subs ever since. Telling her things she would *never* repeat to anyone.

He'd loom over her, threaten her. Every time she'd wonder if that time was when he'd make good on his threats.

Whatever he could do to keep it clear to her that *she* was in his control. That she was powerless.

She wasn't powerless any longer. She wasn't.

Perci also wasn't about to leave Clive Gunderson anywhere near Ivy.

She would not let herself be intimidated by him ever again. She turned her back on him and headed back inside, gambling that he wouldn't do anything to her in broad daylight.

He never had before.

She'd wait until he was gone—or call Joel.

Her brother-in-law could deal with Gunderson far better than she could.

She was tired of giving her energy to this man. It was time she let go of the hold he had on her and moved on.

With Nate.

52

SHE JUST WALKED AWAY. CLIVE WATCHED HER just walk away. As if he, as if *Jay*, didn't matter. He rubbed his hand over his face as he watched her.

Maybe they *didn't* matter to her anymore.

There were others outside, watching. Watching him. Curious.

Gossips, the lot of them. Looking for a show.

He wasn't going to be their damned entertainment.

She shifted again, small and fast and headed to that new baby of Masterson's. He'd scared her away, no doubt.

He hadn't meant to do that. He'd just wanted to *talk* to her. That was all.

Like he hadn't done before.

Clive took another step toward her. Then another. Until he caught up with her. He had her shoulder in his hand before he'd even realized he'd moved. He bodily moved her toward the rear of a pickup truck. Where no one could see.

Perci spun to look at him, a wild fear in those blue, blue eyes of hers.

Had it been the eyes Jay had fallen for first?

She and her twin—all of those Tylers—had those same blue eyes. Hers were big and round, just like her aunt Robin's had been so many years ago.

Clive remembered Robin, too. So many nights he'd thought of *her*. Until Paula.

Hell, Robin had been just a kid the last time he'd seen her twenty years ago. A few years younger than this woman in front of him and hiding behind Perci's father. Telling Clive she didn't want anything to do with him.

Robin had walked away from him, too. "Don't go."

"I have no reason to stay." The girl's tone was cool, uncaring. Because she didn't *care*.

And why should she? She didn't have reason

to care that Jay was dead. Jay had almost killed her. Some said she had scars, didn't they?

For the first time, he wondered how bad those scars were.

She had almost died because of Jay. So why had she lived and his boy not? How was that right? There was another damned version of her walking around somewhere. One of them at least should have died. The fates could have taken one of them and spared his only son. It wasn't right that he'd lost everything and she'd lost nothing. "Yes, you do. You're going to answer my question."

"Let go!" She pulled against his hand. Those eyes shot fire at him. Life.

Damn it, he needed to feel that *life* for a minute.

"No. You're coming with me." Clive tightened his grip and yanked.

He spun her around. She cried out. He just tightened his hold and pulled her into his chest. It was pitifully easy to shove the gun just under her breast.

"If you make another sound, I'm going back inside that diner. You understand me? That deaf sister of yours just walked in with that littlest brother of yours. Not to mention that baby Master-

son's mother was hauling around. You and me...
we're going to go *talk*. Right now."

He dragged her back toward his truck,
knowing his threats toward her family would do
the trick. They always had before.

53

Perci wanted to fight. But she'd seen Phoebe and Parker, too. And Ivy. Ivy was inside. Clive had never physically hurt her before—but he'd just lost his son. He could snap, and she knew it.

If she could just get him away from the diner...

She'd fight like hell to get away from him then.

"Open it." He pushed her toward the door of his truck. Perci complied. Her hand shook, and his grip on her shoulder was far too tight. She finally got the door open. Clive pushed her up the running board and into the cab. He shoved her onto the older bench seat. "Move over."

She thought about sliding out the other side, but he'd follow. And there was nothing to stop Phoebe or Rhea or anyone else from coming outside and looking for her.

Getting right in the middle of everything.

He hadn't moved that pistol away from her since the moment he'd first said her name.

There was no way in hell she was letting him near her family.

54

CLIVE HAD NO IDEA WHERE HE WAS TAKING her. He kept one hand on the wheel and the other on the pistol. She was huddled against the door, looking small and scared.

Making him feel like a total ass. "I'm not going to hurt you."

"Then why did you do this?"

"Life. I need *life*."

"What?"

"Jay's dead. I need to understand why he did it. What is so special about that twin of yours that he'd die to get her? Tell me. Help me understand."

Clive continued to question her as he drove

the miles out toward her daddy's home. Where *his* boy had done something so wrong he'd died for it.

He didn't see the huge, flashy truck that belonged to her boyfriend until it was almost too late.

Clive swerved.

The girl screamed out, calling that damned doctor's name. The hope and fear in her tone echoed through his head.

55

NATE WAS HALFWAY TO HIS HOME WHEN THE old red truck came bulleting around the curve behind him. He swerved, but the truck scraped his side. He yanked the wheel to the right, going off the shoulder.

The truck sped up.

And kept going. Nate pulled over and grabbed his phone. He hadn't been able to see the people inside, but he'd gotten enough of the license plate to funnel that information to his brother.

Tomorrow. Tonight he had important, life-altering plans, and he wasn't about to be derailed because of some scraped paint.

Joel answered his call on the first ring. "Nate? Where the hell are you?"

"Driving out to my place. Some asshole just ran me off the road."

"*Listen.* Clive Gunderson has Perci. He took her from the diner parking lot twenty minutes ago. I need you to get here fast. He's in a red truck, eighties model. Chevy. License..."

Nate interrupted, then rattled off the half of the license plate he'd just gotten, lead filling his gut. "He just ran me off the road. He has her. Just past mile marker forty-eight."

"Don't do anything stupid! We're on our way. I have two choppers about to take off now."

He reached into the glovebox and pulled out the .38 he'd inherited from his father. "Get your ass in one. I'm going after her."

Nate threw his phone on the seat and jerked the gearshift to *drive*.

He floored the pedal and took off after that damned red truck.

56

PERCI'S HAND TIGHTENED ON THE DOOR handle. She bit back another scream when he took the curve just past the turn off to Levi and Pan's home far too fast.

A part of her wanted to just open the door handle and jump. Take her chances and run toward her sister and brother-in-law, and safety.

But at the speed they were going, it was far too risky. She be injured—or outright killed by doing something that desperate. That stupid.

He had to stop sometime.

Nate's truck appeared in front of them, almost by a miracle.

Gunderson cursed. He whipped his older

truck around Nate's. Then they were sliding into the driver's side of Nate's truck. She screamed.

Gunderson yelled again. At her. Told her to shut up.

Perci curled up against her door and prayed. Prayed he hadn't just sent Nate's truck careening off the side of the damned mountain.

She risked turning to see.

His truck was right there. Safe. Thank God, he hadn't careened off the cliff like their car had the night her mother had died.

Wreck Curve Road was just up ahead.

If Clive didn't slow down soon, they were going to go right over the edge.

"Slow down!"

57

CLIVE JERKED THE TRUCK TO THE SIDE AND grabbed his pistol tighter. Masterson was coming up behind him. That damned doctor was not going to ruin this for him.

Not until he got his answers. He wrapped his free hand in the girl's red hair. "Come on. We're getting out. Going to take care of your boyfriend. Then you and I are going to finish this."

She fought. Clawed and snarled like a little kitten. She wasn't much bigger than one, it seemed.

He had a good two hundred pounds on this girl. It was easy to drag her out of the truck. Even with her fighting.

Clive lost his grip on her, and the girl fell to the ground in front of him, landing on her hands in the loose gravel.

Nate Masterson's truck squealed to a stop.

Clive took aim and fired at the center of the windshield.

58

HE DUCKED JUST IN TIME. NATE'S FRONT windshield splintered in front of him. He didn't stop.

"Let her go, Gunderson. My brothers are on their way now. So are the Wyoming Highway Patrol." Nate didn't take his eyes off Gunderson. Nor did he aim the revolver he'd carried in his glovebox away from the other man. "What do you think you're doing?"

"I'm going to talk to her. Find out *why*."

"Why what?"

Perci was on her knees now. Staring at him.

Inching her way toward his truck. To him. So that he could keep her safe.

Gunderson reached for her.

Nate almost pulled the trigger, but Perci was too close. It would be too easy to hit her instead.

There was no way he'd ever risk hurting her.

If Gunderson kept going backward, they'd be at the edge of a thirty-foot drop-off.

Wreck Curve Road, County Rd. 480, was one of the worst in this southern part of the county.

More people had died there than he even wanted to think about. He knew.

He'd had so many of them come through his ER.

Including Perci's mother.

He hadn't been on shift that night, but he'd looked up her medical records after Joel had gotten with Phoebe. Had compared them with what Joel had found in the original accident reports.

Phoenix's car had gone over the guardrail when he'd swerved. It had landed on his mother's side. She'd been in the passenger seat. Perci had been in the rear center. Perci had survived with a concussion, cracked ribs, and the scar on her brow.

The scuff marks were still there on the metal guardrail.

Five feet to the left of where Gunderson stood.

59

CLIVE WANTED TO KILL THE BASTARD RIGHT IN front of him. Just put a hole in the center of the man's chest and get it over with. Do something about how dead *he* felt inside.

He could do it.

Clive had shot three men while he'd been the sheriff; one had lived. He knew how to do it to ensure Masterson didn't live.

It would be so simple.

Red caught the corner of his eye. The girl was moving away from him.

Toward Masterson.

Leaving *him* all alone again.

Clive reached down and grabbed her, dragging her up to her feet.

Masterson was an amateur in gun standoffs. The younger man almost broke cover to get to his girl.

"Don't move, Masterson, or I'll shoot her now."

"What do you think is going to happen?" Masterson yelled back. "Just let her go. *She* has never hurt you. Not even once."

"No?" Hell, he knew that. This girl hadn't even been the one Jay had wanted.

He *just* wanted to talk to her. See if she was as full of the life he remembered from all those nights ago.

Life.

He didn't see much of one for himself any longer.

"No. She hasn't."

He had to give the boy credit. Most people when faced with a man holding a gun to them, and to their girl, would fold. Do whatever he was told, putting himself straight in the control of the gunman.

Not Masterson. Guy was calm and collected—except the one time he looked down at the girl.

Damn it, he hadn't had a woman look at him like that in decades.

Masterson was a damned lucky sonofabitch. That was for sure.

To have a woman with that kind of *life* in her...

"Get over here, girl."

He didn't give her a chance to protest. He lifted her by the shirt. Clive tucked her up tight against his side.

If Masterson got trigger-happy, it wouldn't be Clive he hit.

He imagined it for a half second. The devastation it would cause.

If the girl died.

Like Jay had.

Two entire families would *feel* the pain he felt right then. They'd feel it. All of it. The questions, the hurts, the what-ifs. The knowledge that maybe they could have done something differently and it would have all worked out better.

Masterson especially. "Did you let my son die?"

"No. After stabilizing him that day, I put my best burn trauma staff on him until we could get him to Colorado. It's the best hospital in this region. We did *not* cause him to die. Burn infections are risky from the very beginning. I did not let him die."

"But he's still dead, isn't he? Why?"

"Because of his choices!" the girl hissed at him. Her nails clawed at the arm he now had around her neck. Clive ignored it. He'd been scratched before. He tightened that arm until she gasped.

"Hold still. I'm not finished with him, yet."

Clive heard the chopper headed toward them in the distance.

"Just shut up. I need to think. I just want to know why Jay wanted your sister so bad he'd die for her. I just want to *understand*."

There had to be some meaning in Jay dying and those damned Tyler twins living. There had to be.

60

Perci was trying her best not to panic. His arm kept tightening and loosening on her neck.

He'd jammed his pistol into her ribs and dragged her closer to the guardrail.

The sun cast the shadows over those wooden crosses again.

The shadow from her mother's memorial crossed the toes of her shoes as the clouds overhead shifted to allow more of the setting sun through.

Perci swallowed.

Her mother.

The injuries that had led to her mother's death

had happened not even six feet from where he was dragging her.

If it hadn't been for *his son,* her mother and Phoenix wouldn't have driven in to pick her up that night after she'd worked a double shift.

Her father hadn't let her or her sisters drive anywhere alone at night after Jay had attacked Pip. After *Clive* had threatened them that next day. Her mother had promised to come and get her. Phoenix had gone along so he could *protect* them all.

Instead, Clive Gunderson had almost destroyed her brother, too.

She had never told her father that Clive had found her so many nights and reiterated those threats. Never told. Never asked for help.

Never did anything to stop him.

If she had...

"Let me go, Clive. Now! Just stop this! It's time to stop this!" Perci squirmed as much as she could in his hold.

The chopper with *help* in it was now visible in the distance.

61

NATE WASN'T GOING TO SHOOT GUNDERSON.
Not with the bastard holding Perci so tightly. He
wasn't that good of a shot. He'd never enjoyed it.
Not like Joel and Levi had. The two of them could
hit a walnut off the head of a pin, and had com-
peted as boys to do just that.

But he and Matt hadn't.

All he could hope to do was buy them all some
time for Joel and the WHP to get there. "What
about Clint, Clive? I think he's going through a
pretty bad time right now. Shouldn't he get your
attention now? He needs help."

"He ain't my problem. Never has been."

"He's your son!" Perci said.

Never had she looked smaller to Nate.

"No, he ain't. My brother's boy. I married Paula to give him a name."

Stall. That was Nate's primary thought. To stall. Before that bastard stepped any closer to the edge, or shot Perci. "So he's your nephew. He needs you. He lost his brother, too."

"That's not what this is about. It's about answering my damned questions once and for all!"

"What questions do you have?"

62

HE KNEW WHAT THE BOY WAS DOING. CLIVE wasn't stupid. He'd played the negotiation game himself a thousand times before. This one wasn't experienced at it, but he was better than most. Masterson was good in tense situations, even those with some seriously negative potential consequences.

He held the woman Nate Masterson loved and had a gun shoved in her ribs. And still that boy didn't break down.

The doctor had done a lot of good in the world. Clive had no doubt about that. So had his brother, the vet.

Good men, some said.

He'd heard it during his last bid for reelection. *Mastersons were good men.*

So many had said it, while looking at him and thinking it wasn't true for his son.

Clint, yes. But that boy had more uphill struggles than he could possibly fight. He didn't need Clive cluttering up his way.

After today, he wouldn't need Clive around at all.

He was going to be an embarrassment to Clint, no doubt. Could ruin everything that boy had worked for. His brother a criminal and attempted murderer. His stepdaddy going off the deep end and kidnapping a young woman who had never hurt him like this.

What would that do for Clint's career?

It could potentially destroy everything his stepson had worked for. And it couldn't come at the worst time. Not with Clint and that baby girl of his needing every penny he could bring in.

No one in this town was going to want to have anything to do with Clint and the baby after this.

No one would be able to look at Maria and not snicker and gossip about who she'd let into her bed.

Damn, it would embarrass her. Ruin everything *she'd* built since she'd divorced that bastard who'd liked to knock her around. It had taken him years to get her to trust him at all.

Now she wouldn't trust him at all.

He was going to jail no doubt. With these kinds of cases, *crimes,* there could be extenuating circumstances on account of his recent loss. But he was still facing jail time for the car, for the window, for Masterson's truck.

For taking this girl away at gunpoint.

Everything—his *life*—had just imploded. And he didn't even know why.

He didn't realize he was repeating the question in the girl's ear until he—they—were far too damned close to the edge.

Right next to where her mama had been killed.

"Tell me, Perci. Why did *you* and that sister of yours live, and *my* boy die?"

Clive just needed to know.

To make everything have some sort of *meaning* again.

63

WHY HAD SHE AND PIP SURVIVED? PERCI HAD given it a lot of thought in the weeks since that horrible day when Jay had nearly killed Pip. And her. "Because we were together. I wasn't leaving that barn without my twin, Clive. My sister. My family. I loved her and would do *anything* for her. That day...she ran back into get Jay. To help him, after I was already out. No one chose to leave him in there. We didn't. But *he* chose to try to kill us all. Especially Matt. Because he wanted who wasn't his."

He'd pulled her closer to the edge.

Away from Nate. Nate. She looked at him again.

He'd come out from behind the truck door. Gotten closer. Terror filled her. Clive could just shoot him where he stood, and she wouldn't be able to stop it.

The helicopter was too far away to help them at all. Until it was too late.

"Nate! Get back!" Please, just let him get back.

"I'm not letting him take you one step further, sweetheart. Not without me. Never without me."

"Please, Nate. Just get back behind your truck. Clive's not going to hurt me. Just scare me." She looked around wildly. "It's not even the first time that he's done that in this very spot."

"Let her go, Clive. We're asking you to do that. My brother and her sister didn't *have* to go back in to get Jay. They could have been killed. They almost were. I put the breathing tube down my own brother's throat that day. Same as I did your son. The least you can do is let Perci go. Haven't you terrified her enough?"

Nate kept walking. Kept coming toward her.

"Nate, get *back*. Please! Just get back." Perci clawed at Clive's arm again, trying to break free. Trying to just get to Nate before Clive snapped completely.

64

THE GIRL LOVED HIM. CLIVE COULD HEAR THE desperation in her tone as Masterson just kept walking. *Stupid* of the boy. You never walked toward an armed gunman like that, even if you had a weapon of your own. No matter what the incentive was.

Clive had to admit, a woman you loved in trouble was damned fine incentive though.

He would have walked over hot coals for Maria.

Too bad he had been stupid enough to not realize how he felt about her until it was too late.

"You might want to listen to your girlfriend. I

could kill you right now, then toss her right over the edge."

He never would. He wasn't going to *hurt* this girl. He had never had any intention of hurting her or her sisters. Not even those nights when he'd have a bit of fun with her alongside the highway.

It had always just been something to *do* to feel like he was doing something to help his boy. To protect him.

That twin of hers could have caused some serious trouble for Jay if she'd spoken up four years ago. It would have been much worse for his boy then.

Maybe he'd gone too far. Protected his boy too much.

Hell, maybe if he was still in jail for attacking that twin, Jay would still be alive.

Maybe what had happened would never have happened. Maybe things would be so much different then.

A helicopter soared overhead, drowning out the sound of himself thinking. Another was in the distance. No doubt from the Wyoming Highway Patrol.

Clint would no doubt have heard what was going on by now.

Clive's hand tightened on the girl. She was the only thing keeping those damned kids in the helicopter from putting a bullet in him, he suspected.

He yanked her closer and took another step backward.

The road gave way beneath him.

His hands tightened on her—and on the gun.

The girl crumbled against him, her eyes wide now and filled with pain unlike any he'd seen in a long while—almost before the sound of the gun discharging reached his ears.

He gained his footing on the wet grass and gravel.

The boyfriend yelled her name.

Rushed toward her, not even caring that Clive had the gun.

That Clive could shoot him, too.

He'd shot her. Clive had really shot her.

He'd never forget the sight of those blue, blue eyes staring up at him. His hand was covered with her blood.

She wasn't making a single sound. Not that he could hear, anyway. Over the rush of his own adrenalin and the damned chopper overhead. Of the boyfriend cursing and trying to take her from him.

All Clive had to do was take the gun and shoot that sonofabitch, too.

End it for them all.

End it for Clint. Then they couldn't cause problems for his stepson, that way.

At least he could do that much good.

Sirens were coming. He could see them, maybe. He wasn't so sure. Could hear them. Or was he just imagining them?

Masterson grabbed Clive's gun and yanked it free. He tossed it over the guardrail and down the drop-off. Then he took the girl in his arms.

Bold move on his part. But Clive understood.

Masterson didn't care if he lived or died now. Just that *she* did.

That all of that *life* didn't leave this world, too.

Because of him.

Hands were there, yanking him away from the girl.

Someone rammed his fist into Clive's face.

He just stood there and looked into the face of the patrolman in front of him.

Clint.

Fitting that his stepson was there to see the end of him.

Things had a way of working out the way they were supposed to.

Clive took another step toward the edge, the only thought in his head now of ending it for everyone. Making things easy on the girl, Masterson. Clint. The one person he had left. Clint and the baby.

He should have at least *held* that baby once.

Another step toward the edge.

"Oh no, you don't!" Hard hands yanked him away from the guardrail one more time. Cuffs slapped onto his wrists, and he was secured. Good police procedure.

His first boy always had been the smartest of the Gunderson men. At least Clint would have a better life than Jay. Especially now that Clive wasn't going to be around to mess it all up. He looked at Paula's son, at *his* son, in every way that counted. "I'm sorry, son. I really don't know what happened."

Clint didn't say another word.

He shoved Clive to his knees as Masterson did what he could to keep Perci alive long enough for the air ambulance to land near the police chopper with Masterson's brother nearby.

65

HER SIDE BURNED. HER RIBS. SHE'D HAD broken ribs before. A few times now. Clive's hands were no longer holding her tightly.

But Nate's were. "Nate...I...hurt."

"I know." He turned, putting his body between hers and Clive Gunderson's.

"He's still got the gun..."

"No, honey, he doesn't. The gun went over the cliff. Joel's here. And the highway patrol. Clive's in cuffs. You're safe."

"It went in my side. My ribs. I can't breathe, Nate." Her hand lifted. She just wanted to touch him for a moment. It felt like she was moving through sludge.

She understood about blood loss and shock. They'd had a few gunshot wounds in the ER during her time there—including Joel.

Joel was leaning down next to them. "Honey, it'll be ok. I promise. Hospital is just a few minutes away."

"And here I was hoping to enjoy my day...off. By...seducing...Nate..." All joking aside, her breathing was getting erratic. She could hear it herself. "Nate..."

"Shhh. You're not doing any good by talking. I think it was a through-and-through. Paramedics are coming. We'll get you to Tiff, ok? And Dr. Paterson's on tonight. Then you and I are going to do some talking. Maybe go away for a week or two. I hear Joel knows where there's this little cabin, perfect for me, you, and Ivy. A vacation. Just our little family."

His hands were skilled on her. Confident. But she saw the pain and fear and worry in the eyes she loved so much. Worry for her. "I love you, Nathanial Masterson. Don't you...forget it."

"You're the boss."

He leaned down and kissed her when the paramedics she knew well made it to her side. She tried to concentrate less on the smell of her own blood and the rain and more on the man she loved.

He stepped back to give the paramedics room to get her strapped down, but as soon as they were finished, he was barking out orders at them. Always the man in charge.

Perci smiled. "Quit. They know what they... are doing..."

"You be quiet. Let me take care of you for a change."

She closed her eyes and nodded slightly as one of the paramedics jammed a needle in her arm. Fluids were important, but damn, did it hurt. Her whole body was starting to hurt. Perci closed her eyes as Nate's fingers closed around hers. Then she let herself go, knowing she could trust him to take care of everything.

And he always would. "I love you, Nate. I'll never deny it again."

She heard him say the words right back, then they were strapping an oxygen mask over her face, and she felt herself being lifted.

His fingers never let go of hers.

66

RHEA WAITED AT THE HOSPITAL WITH PIP AND Matt, Levi and Pan, and Phoebe. As well as the rest of the girls' family. Little Parker, who looked so much like Pan it was uncanny, was terrified. They all were.

Ivy was currently sleeping in Phoebe's arms. They'd been passing the little one back and forth while they waited for word.

Rhea checked her watch again. It had been less than an *hour* since Perci had been taken from them.

Less than an hour.

She looked over at Philip as he stormed into

the private waiting room she'd led them all to. "Anything?"

"They're on the air ambulance now." He was pale and shaking. His phone was clutched in his hand. "He shot her. She's hurt. My girl. Gunderson shot her."

Rhea held out her hand. The man she had known for thirty-something years had been through so much hell lately. It wasn't right. "What's her condition? Did they say?"

He shook his head. "I don't know. Signal wasn't good. They're on their way."

All they could do was wait.

Fifteen minutes later, the ER doors burst open. Rhea had been down there waiting, next to Philip. The younger man had needed the support. She knew how much it hurt when your children were injured. It was so different when it was your children.

She saw Joel first, clearing the way for the paramedics. The stretcher was next. Nate came at a run, his hand wrapped around Perci's.

She looked so still and vulnerable.

The hardest thing she had ever done was take that step back and let the ER take care of this woman who meant so much to all of them.

It was hours before she saw Nate again.

When he finally appeared, just what he'd been through showed on his handsome face. He wouldn't have been able to *treat* Perci because of their romantic relationship, but as head of the hospital, he had been granted permission to stay with her the entire time.

"Nate? Honey, how is she?"

"She's going to be just fine. Broken ribs. We had a floating segment or two from the last time. They're fixed now. The bullet struck her liver, but...she's going to be fine. She'll be just fine in time."

Right before her eyes, her strongest, toughest, most reserved son broke down and cried.

All Rhea could do was hold him until he was finished.

When she looked up the rest of their family had surrounded them, wanting news. Rhea looked at Philip first. "She's in recovery. Nate says she'll be just fine."

That's when everyone finally let go of the emotions they'd been holding.

Rhea just kept her hands on her third son and held him as tightly as she could. She understood exactly how the fear of losing the one you loved more than anything else in the world could hurt.

EPILOGUE

WHEN SHE OPENED HER EYES, PERCI KNEW exactly where she was. And who she was with. She'd smelled him before she'd seen him. She would always recognize that unique scent that was him. It was a mix of antiseptic and sexy male that was just always going to be Nathanial Masterson, MD.

His hair stuck up all over his head, but he was wearing clean clothes. Scrubs. From the thin light coming through the window, it was early morning. "Hey..."

She lifted the hand not attached to the IV and touched his hair. He woke and looked at her.

Perci had no doubt he'd slept in that chair next

to her all night. No one would have dared stop him. "What exactly happened?"

"Perci..." He practically breathed her name. "How do you feel?"

"Like Clive Gunderson finally shot me. What happened to him?"

"Clint arrested him, after punching him square in the face. I would have done it myself, but I was more interested in keeping you from bleeding out."

"What's the damage?"

He rattled off the extent of the damage. She winced, and not just from his words. She was going to be feeling what happened for a long while. "I'll recover completely?"

"I'm going to see to it."

She smiled at the way he said it. If at all humanly possible, she believed he'd do it. Her smile faded. "I was so scared. First that he'd hurt Ivy, or your mom, or Phoebe and Parker when they arrived. I didn't know what to do so I just went with him. And he could have killed *you*. I was never so scared in my life until we hit your truck."

A gentle arm slipped behind her. "I was afraid he'd take you from me before I could tell you how I felt. How much of a fool I'd been. I should have just scooped you up the day my mother hired you for me. Gotten all of this out of the way. Joel would have still met Phoebe. Matt would have still met Pip. Levi and Pan would have still made fools out of each other. But I would have had more days with you. I can't forget that."

"I was just as afraid." She pointed to the water on the bedside table. She'd filled and refilled so many of those carafes. The familiar sight of that light-salmon plastic was oddly reassuring.

This hospital was her safe place, and it had been for a very long time.

Here she'd felt free to let go. To fight when she needed to fight.

To fall in love when it was time to fall in love.

To forget everything that had happened since that night Jay Gunderson had changed everything for all of them.

"I'm tired of being afraid all the time, Nate. I'm not going to be afraid anymore. It's over. Clive Gunderson will never be able to hurt us ever again. I want to forget about him."

"If that's what you want, then I'll make it happen."

"Good." She snaked her free hand around his shoulder and tried to guide him closer. He got the message. Then he was leaning in, kissing her lightly. She pushed him away a minute later. Gently. "I have a few more demands, too."

"Lay them on me."

She pulled in as deep a breath as she could without hurting herself. "First. I love you. Second. I'm going to marry you as soon as I can stand up without hurting. Three. We're keeping Ivy. Four. I believe in big families. Five. I'm going to love you forever, no matter how much you argue."

He smiled. "I think I'm up to the challenge. And the answer is *yes*. To all of those."

When he leaned down to kiss her again, Perci kissed him right back.

Everything was *finally* over.

Finally the way it should be.

If you enjoyed this book, please consider returning to your retailer and leaving a review.

Coming from Calle J. Brookes & Lost River Lit Publishing, L.L.C.

WHAT ABOUT CLINT?

Clint has a lot going on right now. It starts in a PAVAD: FBI Case File and concludes in a Masterson County novel. Be sure to read "Buried Secrets: PAVAD: FBI Case File #0005" for more details on just what is happening with Clint and Maggie.

Travis Worthington-Deane was a rancher to his bones and a businessman at heart. The run-down Beise Ranch in Masterson County, Wyoming, eighteen miles away from his business partner Phillip's place, would be perfect to run the specialty cattle operation he had in mind. He would have preferred the ranch be in his native Texas, but he and Phillip Tyler worked well together—and shared the same vision for the herd of cattle they were developing and testing.

It would make them very rich men, if the ten-year experiment paid off.

Or, at least, it would make it *easier* for the two ranchers. Travis was already reasonably wealthy, but that didn't matter to him. What mattered was the family he loved so much.

He hoped that family would grow by a couple kids or so in the next ten years, too.

His new wife was on board with that—and they had had an awful lot of fun practicing the art of baby making since their wedding. A smile flirted at his lips—they'd succeeded, but hadn't shared with the rest of the family just yet. Not yet. It was their secret for a while longer—it was just too new to share.

He turned to her as Phil opened the door to the small, dilapidated barn. "You sure you want to go in there, darlin'? It's dark and spooky. Boogeyman may get you."

Since the terror she'd gone through when they'd first met, Lacy was still a bit frightened of the dark. She was getting better, thanks to therapy sessions at a women's center near the hospital where she worked. But it was still a long process to healing. For all of them.

"I think I'll be able to manage it. Do you think the dog came in here? He didn't look very big."

"*She*. She had teats, darlin'. She's a momma dog."

"Well, we need to find her. *She* looked ragged and abandoned."

And his Lacy wasn't about to leave the dog behind now. Travis smiled to himself. "We'll look for her inside."

"This place has been empty since the twins were in third or fourth grade, I think. The Beises had one around the same age," Phil said. He had a gaggle of kids, all of them redheaded, that he was absolutely devoted to. "About fourteen, fifteen years ago. It's not a large property, but it's ideal for a small herd. We'll need to find someone to watch over the day-to-day."

"You have any ideas?"

"I have a nephew who is looking for a place to stay. Wounded overseas, came home to write books and help his sister with the town bookstore. She writes, as well."

Phil's family stretched from one corner of the

county to the other. They were everywhere. He had a nephew, niece, son, daughter, or son-in-law for just about every need. "He grew up on a ranch with his brothers and sister. He knows what he's doing. Willing to do it for a roof over his head, as long as we pay the utilities until he's settled again. Decides what he wants to do with the rest of his life."

Travis greatly approved of the barter system. And helping family when he could. But he wanted to talk to this nephew first. It was just good business sense, in his opinion. "Definitely something we can consider."

Soft growling sounded when Travis stepped inside the barn. Lots of it. He shifted, putting his body in front of his wife's. "Stay back, honey. I don't know what's in here."

"Quit being overprotective and let me see." Small, feminine hands landed on his back, just above his jeans.

Phil carried a pistol at his hip. He pulled it quietly. Travis pulled his phone free and shined the light toward the rear of the old barn.

Eyes stared back at him—at least six pairs. "Lacy, get out of here. Go wait in Phil's truck."

"Like I'm leaving you behind?"

No. His Lacy wouldn't do that. Travis directed the light at the nearest set of eyes.

"Puppies." The tension left him, and he shifted the light again, counting. "Six."

"What?" Lacy asked.

"She's had a litter of puppies in here." Travis turned and took a step back toward the open door. He shoved it the rest of the way open, illuminating the interior a bit more.

There was the momma dog, right in the center of her little family. Five little bodies growled at them—or at each other as they played.

He heard Lacy's sweet sigh, and he knew... little softie. She wasn't about to leave those puppies behind. No doubt some of those puppies would end up relocated to Finley Creek soon. He hoped his brothers were prepared for the gifts Lacy would give them both.

She'd be talking Phil into taking at least one or two home to his younger boys, no question.

"I suppose Horace does need a wife, too."

Their own beagle, who adored Lacy, was currently having a three-day sleepover with Travis's brother, the governor of Texas. "We can't leave them here. They'll starve."

"There're some cereal bars in the truck," Phil

said softly. "Phoebe made them this morning. I don't think the pups are old enough for solid foods yet. But the mother—"

"She needs help." Lacy stepped closer quietly. She cooed tenderly, patiently. Until the momma stepped toward her. Lacy looked at Travis. "The cereal bars?"

Travis knew what she wanted. He fetched like the good husband he was.

Fifteen minutes later, Lacy was cuddling the momma and giving her a cursory inspection, while getting licked in return. Travis and Phil had been relegated to puppy catchers. Phil had a small kennel in the back of his truck that he'd used to ferry his daughter Phoebe's goats to the vet—his son-in-law Matt—a few days earlier. It came in handy.

Travis was chasing the last of the furry little boogers around when his foot tangled in an old bundle of rags—and he went crashing to the ground.

He couldn't help himself.

Travis screamed like his niece Katie whenever she saw a spider.

Phil and Lacy came running. The momma dog barked her fool head off, her puppies mimicking her immediately.

"What in the hell, Deane?"

"Keep Lacy back!" Travis yelled at the older man, who immediately blocked Lacy from seeing the grisly sight Travis knew he would never forget.

A human skull stared back at him, a macabre grin on its face.

Travis fought the urge to vomit.

He looked at Phil. "You'd best call the sheriff. We just found a body, and I don't think it put itself here."

Phil's curse echoed in the barn around them.

Travis stood and went to his wife. He knew she'd seen human remains before—she was an ER doctor, after all—but this was a sight he didn't want her to see in her nightmares. She already had enough nightmares of her own.

Officer Jim Hollace with the Wyoming State Police listened to the call out as it went over the radio, reporting a body found. And he *knew*.

That address still haunted him. Still came into his nightmares. He drove by there almost every day he worked, just to see. To remember.

He'd done some stupid things fourteen years ago. Shit that hadn't left him alone since. In his job, he'd seen the worst of humanity. Beer and bourbon did very little to block it out. He'd tried. Lost two wives and three kids because of it.

That address, that woman, had always haunted him. Probably always would.

He circled the block—he was assigned the region just next to the Masterson region. He'd tried to stay away from Masterson and the ranch where he'd lived for a few years, but, sometimes, it just pulled him back.

Sometimes, he went out there and just sat, drinking away the memories.

Jim snorted. The memories never went away. Far from it.

Like her ghost was keeping him there or something.

Which was stupid.

He hadn't done anything but try to protect his family. Luther's kids were his cousins, too. Step, but still family. He had to remember that.

He'd tried to make up for what had happened. He'd sobered up a bit then, dropped the drugs. He hadn't touched a single drug since those days. He was proud of that.

Jim had been lucky to have never gotten busted with anything other than a beer or two. The Wyoming State Police had been able to brush underage drinking off. Jim had had the connections, thanks to his cousin Luther's friendship with the then-sheriff of Masterson, to make certain nothing stayed on Jim's record. He'd gotten a good job with the Wyoming State Police, and he knew it. He'd done his best.

He'd done his best.

That was all he could say.

But Masterson still haunted him. Damned town probably always would.

They'd just found one of the ghosts he'd longed to forget.

He had to get home. Get himself something to drink. Something to help him forget.

Jim drove his patrol car just a little too fast on the county roads until he got there.

Sheriff Joel Masterson looked at the body as the state forensics team worked diligently to uncover it. It was his county, but it being a murder—because no one wrapped themselves up in a pink and orange quilt and buried themselves in Luther Beise's barn by accident—made him glad he'd made the decision over the phone to have the Wyoming Division of Criminal Investigation called in as soon as possible. Joel knew what he was capable of, and he knew what resources his little squad actually had. He could handle the case —but it would pull resources from areas that he didn't want to stretch right now.

They were always stretched thin—in both manpower and monetary resources. It was just the way it was for his office. He'd known that going in. He had six deputies, now.

It was just bad luck that the *one* DCI agent sent into help was the one Joel wanted nowhere near Masterson County.

There had always been a bit of political jockeying about jurisdiction on the big cases since he'd been elected, but he was working on fixing the chasm that the previous sheriff had created.

Seemed like all Joel did any more was clean up the previous sheriff's messes. Those messes just kept coming to the surface when he least expected it. Joel damned Clive Gunderson for nothing less than the four hundredth time.

His thoughts darkened further when he

thought of his wife's younger sister—*his* brother Nate's wife—and how she'd almost died at Clive's hands.

It would take a long, long time to forget that.

He looked at Clive Gunderson's stepson and fought the snarl.

Too many memories Joel wanted to forget. His sister-in-law's blood all over the side of the road, for one thing. The terror on Nate's face was another. He'd never had a real problem with Clint before, but just the sight of him hurt now.

It was the first time their paths had crossed since Clive Gunderson had nearly killed Perci. Hard to forget Clint had been there that day, too.

"There's a letter in her pocket," the state crime scene tech said. "It still has a date on it."

The tech read it aloud quickly. Fourteen years. The letter was dated fourteen years ago. If it had been in the ground that long, it was a miracle it had survived intact. Considering what had been... decomposing...around it. "The date and name are about all that's legible. For now. We'll have someone process it. See if they can figure out what it says, and if it's significant."

Joel's stomach turned. He no doubt knew the victim in some way. In a county this small, it was hard not to know just about everyone in some way or another.

Clint walked over to him. "Luther Beise was an associate of Clive's. A cousin on his mother's side. They were good friends."

"I remember. I was in college at the time, but my brothers kept me informed of what went on around here." Luther Beise had had a reputation as an isolationist around Masterson. The family's sudden disappearance had just fueled those stories. Rumors had ranged the entire gamut—from alien abductions to a mass homicide carried out by Luther himself. With bodies everywhere on the ranch. Teenagers sometimes went hunting for those bodies of the Beises'.

Clint had been on sight twenty minutes before Joel had been able to get there.

"I've been going over Clive's files. When this address came over the wire, I asked for the case. Clive tried to find the Beise family for a few years. Then he abruptly stopped looking, and the file stopped. I don't want my name attached to it, not alone, but I want to follow this trail where it leads. It...might tie into others I'm investigating. If you work the case with me, people won't object as much."

No surprise. Clive Gunderson had probably not wanted to put in the work at the time the Beise family had left.

Or he had been too busy harassing people like he had the Tylers.

There was no way Joel wanted to partner up with Clint. No doubt that was what was about to happen, though. "So what's got you spooked about this?"

"Clive named names that are still...relevant. A case I'm working on is bigger than a single dead woman. It's complicated. I don't need eyes in my direction now." Gunderson's voice dropped. "I... am trying to untangle everything Clive did. But if something happens to me, I want...a friend...with the FBI to know what's going on. She was friends with the elder Beise sister. I've already called her department and spoken with her superiors. She'll be pulled to work with us—if we request it down the road."

"You're expecting something to happen to you?" Joel sent a look Clint's way.

The guy was serious.

The man was probably as bat-shit crazy as his father and brother had been. Joel couldn't overlook that possibility.

"Who knows? Some of what I'm finding, Masterson, it's not good. Just...if something happens to me, you make sure my baby girl is kept safe."

Gunderson had an infant daughter he was raising on his own. That he'd brought her into the conversation had Joel's gut tightening.

Gunderson might be bat-shit crazy, but he believed what he was saying. If he wasn't off his rocker, then something more was brewing.

"I know it's a lot to ask. But there're not a whole lot of people out there I still trust any longer. I know you're honest. And you'll do the right thing when needed. You make sure my baby girl stays with the woman who loves her the most. No matter what. The woman who loves her the most. You'll know who that is, if the time comes."

Joel just nodded. Something about the look in the man's eyes had his skin crawling. "You think whatever you have going on here is related to what we've found?"

"I wouldn't, except for the fact that Luther Beise was one of Clive's old cronies, and there was more going on with that bastard than anyone ever expected. I'll be paying for the sins of that man for a long, long time to come. Least I can do is make certain what he did isn't still hurting people."

Joel just grunted. What Clint was saying was the truth—the entire town of Masterson had practically turned against Clint after what Clive had done to Perci and the rest of her family.

It wasn't right. Clint hadn't done a damned thing to anyone that Joel knew about.

Joel should probably make that known when he could. Show the town he had no hard feelings personally against the younger man.

Clint just had the bad luck to be related to Clive.

"We'll do what we can. And if it comes time to call in the feds, I'll make room for them without a problem. I don't care who finds the killer—I just want the killer found."

Joel wouldn't hold Clive's actions against another man. Joel considered himself a better man than that. He would just keep reminding himself of that when the need arose.

Clint was called away, leaving Joel to think about what the man had said.

If this was related to Clive Gunderson, Joel wanted the outside eyes on things, too. He and Clint—they were too close to this, and with the history between their families, the objectivity would cover all their asses.

ALSO BY CALLE J. BROOKES

ROMANTIC SUSPENSE

PAVAD: FBI ROMANTIC SUSPENSE

Falling

Hiding

Seeking

FINLEY CREEK SERIES

TRILOGY ONE (TEXAS STATE POLICE)

Her Best Friend's Keeper

Shelter from the Storm

The Price of Silence

TRILOGY TWO (FINLEY CREEK GENERAL)

If the Dark Wins

Wounds That Won't Heal

Hope for Finley Creek (bonus novella)

As the Night Ends

TRILOGY THREE (FINLEY CREEK DISASTER)

Before the Rain Breaks

Lost in the Wind

Walk Through the Fire

MASTERSON COUNTY NOVELLA SERIES

Seeking the Sheriff

Discovering the Doctor

Ruining the Rancher

Denying the Devil

SMALL-TOWN SHERIFFS

Holding the Truth

SUSPENSE/THRILLER

PAVAD: FBI CASE FILES

PAVAD: FBI Case Files #0001

"Knocked Out"

PAVAD: FBI Case Files #0002

"Knocked Down"

PAVAD: FBI Case Files #0003

"Knocked Around"

PAVAD: FBI Case Files #0004

"White Out"

PAVAD: FBI Case Files #0005

"Buried Secrets"

Calle has several free reads available at

www.**CalleJBrookesReads.com**

For my grandfather, the best man I have ever known.

You will be missed.

Oct. 2015

For my grandmother, who gave me the courage to try.
Without you and your love of romance, I never would
have made it this far.

Feb. 2016

For my papaw, whose children loved him deeply, and
will always miss him.

Oct. 2017

Calle J. Brookes enjoys crafting paranormal
romance and romantic suspense. She reads almost
every genre except horror. She spends most of her time
juggling family life and writing while reminding herself
that she can't spend all of her time in the worlds found
within books. CJ loves to be contacted by her readers
via email and at **www.CalleJBrookes.com**. When
not at home writing stories of adventure and wrangling

with two border collies and a beagle puppy, CJ is off in her RV somewhere exploring the beautiful world we live in, along with her husband of she can't remember how many years and their child.

REED652020